Through the Woods

Through the Woods

Martha Lee

THROUGH THE WOODS
Copyright © 2021 by Martha Lee

All rights reserved. No part of this publication may be reproduced, distributed, or transmitted in any form or by any means, including photocopying, recording, or other electronic or mechanical methods, without the prior written permission of the publisher or author, except in the case of brief quotations embodied in critical reviews and certain other noncommercial uses permitted by copyright law.

Although every precaution has been taken to verify the accuracy of the information contained herein, the author and publisher assume no responsibility for any errors or omissions. No liability is assumed for damages that may result from the use of information contained within.

Library of Congress Control Number: 2021925125
ISBN-13: Paperback: 978-1-64749-674-6
                ePub: 978-1-64749-675-3

Printed in the United States of America

GoTo Publish
GoToPublish LLC
1-888-337-1724
www.gotopublish.com
info@gotopublish.com

To the memory of my late grandmother, Ruthella Chaplin Lee, who inspired and encouraged my passion for writing.

The lone soul shuffling along the beach was no sleepwalker. Though lost in thought, nothing escaped her attention. All things touched by the sea turned to magic. The surf, bearing new treasures, rolled in to greet her like a friendly pup.

She stopped often to inspect some intriguing find. She filled her hands with seashells, touched the shiny knobs of seaweed floating in like vain snakes. She saw a jumbled trail of crab claws strewn in the scavengers' wake and jerky-strutting sandpipers jab at the sand in search of hidden tidbits.

A stray mutt romped toward her, just close enough to flaunt a dead gull hanging from its snout.

She watched greenhorn riders cling to the reins as their horses clomped along the shore. A few sat bolt upright but awkward bouncing belied their brave fronts.

She spotted swarms of people down the beach in a tangle of strings, streamers, bizarre fish, fan and plane shapes wildly patterned and colored. It was a buzzing mix of contenders and curious locals, amassed for the annual kite festival.

She found abandoned sandcastles filled and fallen with seawater; driftwood forts, posting squatters' rights, warned potential invaders.

It was all the flowing retreats, ebbing arrivals, pulsing, spewing, pounding—of life by the sea.

She absorbed it all, even while in the midst of pondering her past, present and future.

She remembered how yesterday, as she fled to the ocean, rain sloshing ruthlessly against the van's windshield, her old twinge returned about driving in the rain. The early darkness hadn't helped. It was cold, dark and rainy, typical for a northwest December day. But her spirits rallied briefly when she thought of its wild natural beauty on the rare good days.

Daydreaming as usual going rotely down that familiar freeway stretch, she was alerted abruptly to the Ocean Beach turnoff. Leaving the main road to get onto the narrower, crowdless beach road, she sighed in relief, then drifted back into her thoughts.

Sure of only one thing—that she was headed to the beach—she shivered with expectancy. To be by the sea, her thoughts and feelings flowing as freely as the tide coming onto the shore, intoxicated yet soothed her and was essential for her peace of mind.

She knew from experience that if feeling out of kilter or vaguely disoriented on the way, order and peace came mysteriously within reach upon arrival. There were the uplifting rituals of walking through the sea town streets, sampling homemade soup and pastry at a small café table by the window. Every inch of the town was steeped in sea air, seasoning its magic.

Along the way the tension-demon began retreating from her limbs. Stress worked its way from between her shoulders, down along her arms then out through her fingertips. The unwinding process had begun. Stretching luxuriously, she felt relaxed, like some lazy sated jungle cat after a successful kill.

She knew that threadbare road, bumpy and dimly lit, almost by heart. She'd been over it since childhood with family and others. They'd stayed in cramped, weathered cabins for those short boisterous vacations together with dogs, utensils, beach toys, tangled stacks of socks, scarves, old shoes, jackets, hats, and gloves. Yearly that caravan of paraphernalia, owners in tow, headed to the beach.

More trips followed with school friends, then with one very special friend. Then later with another friend and later still, alone. The times alone had been best. Those times had been filled with a solitude made more profound by the sound of breaking surf faintly roaring through her cabin walls. Alone, she wandered for miles along the nearly vacant beach, imprinting the pudding-like sand with her toes. Sitting staring for hours into infinity, she followed the flight of the seagulls up, over, down. Raptly curious, she studied the solitary figures lost in private musings among the rocks, driftwood, and dune grass. Those sacred rituals she held tightly to her . . . .

Suddenly snapping to, she had slowed the van as she neared a tiny town of one café, one gas pump and one house, undoubtedly the café owners. Inside the café several locals, presumably workers from nearby logging sites, milled about, then congregated at the counter where a barman took orders. The dark room, large and open, was scattered with tables, chairs and other rough-hewn furniture. Cedar planks lined the walls. The interior and almost every occupant, herself included, were imbued with a natural rusticity.

A tall, bearded man in a plaid logger's shirt jauntily swaggered toward her. His sharp, rugged face was flushed. When he spoke to her it was in a tone filled with a drink-inflated sense of his own importance.

"How 'bout joinin' me for a drink. It'll take the chill off your bones," he'd ventured. Boldly his eyes surveyed every inch of her anatomy.

A glint like those found in starving wild animals pierced his eyes. His hungry glance struck her as finding her all too appetizing. Standing her ground, she looked calm and distant. But inside she was grinding, grating, seething to a boil. Her instincts told her that potential danger stood before her. Signals inside her head warned: *Don't go any nearer.* The bright red flashes blinked on and off with rapid urgency. *The man spells trouble—stay away.*

And Hattie, surprising herself by hearing and, for once, heeding her inner instinctive voice, bolted.

Right then, only two things concerned her—the women's room and the gas pump. The van was almost empty, as usual, a greedy guzzler of the worst kind that, luckily for its own sake, had redeeming qualities.

She made her way down a dank, dusty corridor to the restroom. Neglected and stagnant, it was little more than a dingy cubicle.

Fresh air was her most pressing concern. Charging out the front door and into the night, she had been hit by the bracing night chill. No stars softened the dark sky.

Like other lone souls before and millions to come, she made her pilgrimage to the ocean to forget. She came to patch up her ravaged heart's wounds with an infallible old healer known as sea air. Though inconsolable at the time, some inner force magnetically swept her on toward that most terrible, majestic, fathomless of all mysteries.

Back on the road again, the face of her lover—the man she'd left in the city—had floated into focus causing her to wince and squirm with pain. It was a face so intimately vivid that every mark, crease and contour was stamped across her brain forever.

His eyes are smiling, now grinning, now they're laughing, questioning, cajoling, pleading-cat-eyes that can break with cunning quickness from a lazy, mischievous glint into a lusty chuckle—the eyes of a sun-drenched lion splayed out on warm granite waking playfully to the prospect of stalking prey.

They'd begun badly. She, very low the day they met, vulnerable, gloomy; he, buoyant, pressing, closing in. She hadn't wanted the kitten he'd given her, hadn't wanted the crowd they'd mingled with, hadn't for certain wanted him either. She'd taken him in a wrangling, tangled night of sheer lust, but it hadn't sated her, had left her feeling empty, lonelier than before.

Afterward, his body turned from her, she'd cringed into a ball of despair. It had been a fitful night, unfamiliar. In the morning he'd flippantly wangled his way back into her. A sense of oppression had crept through her again only sharper than it had been through the veil of drink and darkness.

Hattie recalled roaming through the stranger's house trying to infiltrate him as if to strike back at the bewildering intensity of their union.

Who is he, this man already weaving a spell over me and WHAT is this aura of intrigue emanating from him?

She was very curious and it was then that she'd begun her mission to decipher his code.

His room was very small, barely wide enough to accommodate the double bed and chest of drawers facing it. The walls were the color of a robin's egg, the doors and moldings trimmed in white. A small, red, white and black patterned Mexican blanket draped the closet door. A rag rug lay on the floor beside the bed and the only window was set high and opened in, held by a chair on either side. One light, softly-patterned blanket lay crumpled on the bed. Ski, climbing and fishing gear mingled with camping utensils and a bicycle virtually obscured the walls. The dresser top held a can of lighter fluid, small change, a watch, ashtray, pocketknife and an unframed photograph of him kneeling beside a sandy blonde-haired woman wearing glasses. They were smiling.

Hattie sauntered into the living room. He whistled in the kitchen, making coffee. Tan leather furniture and frayed, overstuffed chairs faced a smoke-stained, white-washed brick fireplace. The mantle-top was stacked with magazines, loose papers and utility bills. Sophisticated stereo equipment sat on plywood planks held up by bricks. A neglected looking plant hung drooping from a dingy macramé basket hooked to the ceiling.

He handed her a cup of coffee as she followed him to the kitchen where he poured cream in both cups. She liked that room. It was sunny, cheerful and had a familiar, intimate feel, like her grandmother's kitchen, stuffed with miscellaneous utensils, painted cookie jars, spice bottles. The back door, glass-paned on top, was open, letting in the August sunlight. It was going to be hot.

Eyeing him across the table she shivered from the strange electric current passing through her. She stared into her coffee cup in a feeble effort to hide her angst. Some-thing about him stirred a long dead place inside her. Even sitting, he was charged, aglow with earthy, intense vitality. Yet the underside of the curious, brazen beast, slightly tilting his lion-like head, conveyed a mystified, lackadaisical nonchalance.

Going out for breakfast, their steps fell in sync. He was intrigued his eyes said. Though she couldn't quite crystallize it, she sensed that his well-honed instincts found something unbridled, even volatile, in her.

His glance mirrored his appraisal:

She looks like some wild jungle cat with her dark, unruly hair, those eyes flashing with such intensity like a panther slinking through the underbrush-spirited, temperamental, sensuous, responsive, untamable—a challenge . . .

She sensed his preoccupation was due to a scathing dissection of her. She railed at the notion of him sizing her up, categorizing, manipulating her essence in any way. He saw her stiffen and started tackling the bleak looking food in front of him.

She poked insults at the instant oatmeal, the frozen orange juice, the watery, instant eggs and coffee, could hardly force them down. They talked, haltingly, like the strangers they were, revealing little.

Suddenly he left for a sailing race with a crew waiting for him in a small northern port town. She camouflaged her disappointment, wanting to uncover more. She felt suddenly let down, slightly despondent knowing she would be alone again. The unabated loneliness, always deep inside, was so much a part of her that she had stoically grown to accept it.

Driving home, she pulled onto one of the ugliest stretches of concrete in the city. Jammed with early morning commuter traffic, it was an appalling, chaotic jumble of poles, wires, billboards, neon signs, all-night diners, dilapidated motels, abandoned gas stations. Maneuvering in and out of the frenzied crush, she cringed with repulsion at each passing horror. Her spirits lifted slightly as she glimpsed the lake outlined by a running path and clumps of willows. A bit further she passed the zoo, a dense thicket, rolling hills, marshes, meadows, dotted with wildlife—two urban oases, the only bright spots along the endless strip of visual obscenity.

Relieved to be home, she kicked off her shoes, ran a tub of scalding water and soaked her limbs until she felt limp as a rag.

Video-like, the events of the past twenty-four hours flitted before her. An entire scenario ran its course from beginning to end. It was the story of a doomed relationship, echoing her own gloomy forecast for it. Nothing concrete could come of the sensual marathon, the wild, even violent battles of will and stormy scenes of recrimination. End-less rifts and reunions ordained by different needs; two fighters struggling toward self-hood and independence. She wrapped her arms around her knees hugging them to her, a defensive reflex prompted by the thought of compromising either solitude or serenity.

Her innermost spirit was and always had been free. She guessed the man was free too, independent, adventurous, soulful. His name was Murdoch. That was the only name she'd ever heard him called. They'd come together, drawn by a powerful animal attraction stronger than either could ignore or resist. It seemed destined.

Foreseeing the inevitable, a shiver, ran through her and she stung with sadness. Somehow, as never before, she despaired of ever having solidity or permanence. Already, like the sea at low tide, the intensity of their bond was waning.

He called two days later asking to see her. All rational thought left her. Her senses took charge and she heard herself accepting. But her instincts registered trepidation and skepticism. Dual wills were at work within her. One said yes with bravado, the other to be careful. They started seeing each other, seldomly at first, then more often. His past began to unfold but the more he unraveled, the less her curiosity was quelled. His marriage had shattered long before and though separated, neither had filed for divorce. He wanted to be free of his wife's strangulating domesticity, but couldn't seem to sever the ties mostly because of his two children. He felt bound to them in his fashion, but emotionally unequipped to stay. Hattie sensed his despair, the stigma he attached to having failed them. Coming from a similar situation only childless, she empathized, shared his pain, his floundering state. But she felt her own pain, the times he seemed so far away, lost in his plight. Often he reached out for her and let her into his world, but her ache of loneliness was unassuaged. Too frequently he was with them, physically as well as in spirit. Once he attempted a reconciliation but to no avail. Hattie, devastated, received him back. Nothing between them was ever quite the same again. His loyalties were too divided, too vague. Traumatized, she formed a veneer of indifference, an envelope of distancing, while aching deeply for him to be completely there. They continued an intimacy lacking substance or direction. For her, it was a more frustrating sensation than she'd ever known. She shrank from expanding or developing her involvement. Her needs surpassed his desire or capacity to deliver. He resisted, then advanced. She received and retreated. They ebbed and flowed, stood still and backed away. Each was grappling with a quagmire of expectations.

A massive overhaul of the ramshackle house she's bought just before meeting Murdoch was in progress. He pitched in, recruiting a small band of craftsman friends.

The house, larger than it looked from the outside, had two stories plus a full daylight basement. Cedar-shaked, it was fronted by a long, narrow porch and four square posts. It reminded her of an oversized beach cottage, rustic with open, airy interior rooms, battered wood floors and beamed ceilings. A used brick mantle, slate hearth and new fireplace replaced the original metal insert, so she could have roaring fires, one of her greatest pleasures.

First, they tackled the foundation, shoring up, ripping out dry rot, knocking out ceilings, walls and doors. A cement floor was poured and leveled, a tiny bath installed in place of the dingy, step-up latrine. She designed a set of solid fir steps, having them built to replace the rickety, rotted old ones. Held together by huge bolts, they had a bold, industrial look. The kick-boards were omitted to let in maximum light. She felt very satisfied with the handsome, sound results.

Her solitude was shattered by the crew trampling in, out, up and down. She hardly had any peace for days at a time. She made major decisions, directed traffic, paid wages and suppliers. Tempers flared, petty grievances, rifts and bruised egos cropped up among the workmen. She was relieved when Murdoch was there. He had a knack for smoothing ruffled feathers that she often lacked. He had an easygoing camaraderie with the men, but occasionally two of them would butt heads like a pair of rutting bulls, stomping, huffing and stalking off.

Murdoch kept irregular hours, disliking the early hours and growing increasingly restless after too long in one place. He craved being on the move. It was in his blood like a raging disease and he appeased it by roaming off alone, usually to some backwoods bar to belt down a few beers, or pitchers, depending on his mood. She knew of these bouts, had gone with him more than a few times. At first it had been an amusing adventure, something to do, somewhere to go, a chance to spend more time with him. She entertained herself by recording the minutiae of objects and bodies around her, or watching Murdoch play video games and pool. Morose at times, he'd sit staring into his glass, times she couldn't reach him. He seemed to be ticking off his losses, all the lost chances, lost loves, time wasted. He wallowed in self-pity and remorse, barely aware of her presence, inconsolable, untouchable.

The restoration work was grueling. Jack-hammering the basement slab into chunks, then unloading it in dozens of wheelbarrow loads in a dumpster took back-breaking days of labor. It was too thin and flimsy to hold the new support beams under the sinking west side of the house and had crumbled under the weight of the pole jacks raising the structure. The extent of work to be done unnerved her and the drills yammering incessantly broke her concentration.

Murdoch failed to show on time the day the cement truck arrived. When he finally straggled in, Hattie had already carted several piles of gravel to the site and unloaded them. It was very annoying but there wasn't time to waste on recriminations. The machinery and materials were assembled and ready. Wet cement came gushing through an enormous hose and flooded the dirt floor. Slavishly, furiously, the men strained, struggled to keep pace with the incoming rush of spewing gray goo. Paving with quick, wide sweeping motions, they mowed the ground with liquid concrete. Bending and swaying, monkey-like, they scrambled to disperse the mixture evenly. Finally, the pump stopped. It was not completely spread and leveled until late that night. Worn out, they were relieved when it was over. The fire being the only source of heat, Hattie and Company, huddled, shivering, near it to unthaw, ravenously gulping down hot buttered rums. All the antiquated radiators had been pulled out. So had the dilapidated gas-powered boiler with fat, asbestos-covered, octopus arms. Before the fireplace was installed she could remember the times the house was as cold inside as it was out, the only heat coming from a small kerosene burner. At every chance, she gravitated to the fire, the soul of the house, the source of all light and warmth.

Sitting in front of it, staring into the flames, voices buzzing in the background, her spirits had lifted. She was feeling more relaxed and content than she had for ages.

Murdoch watched her. His eyes grilled into her back, but she stayed still. He wanted her but she seemed unattainable, an essence hovering just beyond his reach, striving, seeking some unknown.

What is she after? Is it solace, tenderness? Or is it pleasure, adventure, passion, intrigue?

He knew gentleness, had shown it to her, shared it, touched her with it. She had opened to him, naked, vulnerable. She had also stung him with her deadly tongue. Cringing, he knew how protective she was of her own territory. Her colossal thirst for independence, like his, was staggering. She spewed her wrath when he treaded too heavily, came too close. Infringement, she insinuated. She slapped him once in a rage of frustration, of tears and reprisal. The storm of pent-up tension broke after he plunged through a wall while yanking out an obsolete drainpipe. She saw red, felt it was sheer carelessness, another instance of his clumsy indifference. Inconsolable, venting recriminations, she forced him out, away. He stomped off in silence.

Guilty, she summoned him through one of the crew. She knew she needed him to do the work. He worked hard and fast and helped relieve some of her burden. He came back to a painful reunion, both of them fiercely proud. They worked on, completely stripping the main rooms, removing old sheet rock, wiring, plumbing pipes. Since he was intent on doing some fly-fishing, they decided to take a break. He heard it was good in the Colorado River, in the basin of the Grand Canyon so he asked her to go with him. She said yes but thought the idea both preposterous and compelling. It was November, good fishing season. He helped her make out a list of supplies they would need, most of which she had to borrow, until everything was gathered together and they started out.

They were finally on the road and it felt good.

The further they drove from the cities and towns into sparser, vast regions of barren land and starkly silhouetted rolling hills, the more Murdoch opened up as he surveyed his surroundings. He talked in abstracts, letting ideas drift and flow like the passing landscape. He was in a private dream world, populated by pioneers, covered wagons, Indians, bands of raiders, bows and arrows, big game herds, unsullied rivers; a land untouched by man—wild, free, untamed, extinct.

Once, in the midst of her reverie, his voice drifted to her from the distance. "You and I commune not so much on the ordinary everyday level of understanding, but on a higher plane of consciousness," in a feeble attempt to reassure her they belonged together. She, always surprised by the meager revelations into his depths, being so scarcely touched on, thought how little indeed they had to share. She remained unconvinced because on some more profound level he was not digging deeply enough into her essence, leaving her feeling lonely, restless and confused. Tormenting waves of ambivalence toward him washed through her incessantly, charging her with agitation. His dormant will, when aroused, forced itself against, her, threatening her resolve.

They cut across the southern tip of Idaho, slashing through the belly of Utah, past hundreds of miles of low, barren, purple hills. The simplicity of their soft contours was pronounced against the pale, cloudless sky. For Hattie, used to great forests, it was a strangely moving sight, stirring in her an ache of sadness.

In Arizona, skirting the Painted Desert, wildflowers and low lying shrubs proved the only spots of color. The desert signaled they were almost there. The canyon's massive expanse loomed up ahead meeting them with an onslaught of magical beauty. It splayed before them like a huge paint-splashed crater, striated with giant bands of assorted color. They were the primitive shades of adobe, reeds, hemp, jute-rich earthy tones intensified by the sun.

The first night they camped out near the descent trail, spreading the sleeping bag out in the back of the wagon. Early the next morning, when they drove to the large parking area above the trail, a storm was blowing in from the North Rim, gusting furiously. Rain, snow pelts and freezing wind pounded down, swirling around the car, semi-obscuring anything more than a few feet away, making their attempts to add extra pieces of warm clothing—boots, hats, gloves—twice as difficult.

Finally, their packs and gear strapped in place, they trudged over to the trail crest and started the trek down. Almost as soon as they began the descent, Hattie noticed an increase in temperature. The trail, protected by the surrounding canyon walls, was dry and sun-warmed with no sign of the storm they had left behind, raging at the higher elevation. The trail was gradual at first, and easy, cutting through grassy meadowland sprinkled liberally with wild mountain flowers, scrub-brush and an assortment of desert-like shrubbery. Even at this level, they could see far down into the canyon to its floor. Glancing down, she thought the sight below her more magnificent then anything she'd ever seen. A shiver of awe swept over her, causing a momentary chill as she peered down to the muddy green ribbon of the Colorado some seven miles below.

Murdoch set a rapid pace. To him, an experienced climber, muscular, with tremendous stamina, this trek looked to be child's play. He was eager to reach the river, to get some fishing in before dark. For Hattie, the shock of realizing that with twenty-five extra pounds on her back she could not sustain the pace hit hard. She wanted to stay with him, share the time with him, but she was already painfully aware that he wouldn't wait, wouldn't be held back. He was obsessed, driven to conquer the unknown terrain, pushing ahead, relentless. She stubbornly maintained her own pace, fell behind, eventually losing sight of him. She railed against his incessant restlessness. Let him miss the glory around them, but she intended to revel in it, absorb it into her very core. It was the closest she'd been to a spiritual oasis and she wasn't willing to relinquish a moment of the euphoria of exploring an earthly paradise.

Traversing down a series of switchbacks, she spotted Murdoch, a mere speck in the distance. Only his movement alerted her, so like a chameleon that at a standstill he would have blended without a trace into the surroundings.

Gingerly making her way down the steep incline, her mind strayed back to their stay several nights before at a remote spot called Lee's Ferry.

They'd set up camp on a bluff directly above the Colorado. It was still light when they arrived. Murdoch grabbed his fishing pole and he and Hattie set out for the river. On the way they came to a creek too wide for Hattie to cross without getting soaked. Murdoch, waterproof in his waist-high waders, hoisted her on his back as if she were light as a feather and plunged into the stream. She remembered how the riverside had been lush with tall reed grass and a vast thicket of trees. Instinctively she was drawn to the river, something thrilling and terrifying in the sound of its crashing roar. Something deep and mysterious in its murky green depths held her spellbound, its churning tempo keeping pace with her own inner rhythm.

Murdoch was excitedly thrashing with something snagged on the end of his line. Reeling it in and putting it up to inspect, they saw it was no ordinary fish but exotic looking, thick-lipped with multi-colored markings. The upper lip was almost snout-nosed, curved and slightly hooked out over the bottom one. Murdoch was stumped, never having seen one like it. It almost looked like a strange brand of dogfish, but he had the feeling it might be a rare breed. He let it go, catch-and-release style, being satisfied with the thrashing battle it had waged against him. After that he caught and kept several trout for their dinner.

They were back at the campsite in time to watch the sun set beyond the river, lighted a fire and began the preparations for dinner. The day's drive and the fishing had put them both in an easy, mellow mood. An intensely peaceful aura emanated from the wilderness around them. As they watched the sky darkening with dusk, turning an electric blue, a stillness settled over everything, still but charged with an ineffable vibrancy.

That night, after gorging themselves on fresh trout and washing their utensils, sitting by the campfire they watched a star-studded sky, the moon reflected on the river and she felt closer to Murdoch than ever before. Some strange bond linked them, something primeval, a tenacious rapport that each of them was secretly nurturing. They seemed to be communing on interchangeable levels, one an elevated plane, lofty, meshing in a subconscious trance-like state; the other instinctive, the natural, sensuous realm of primitive passions.

They came to each other with a secret awareness of the deepening intimacy between them. Their mutual desire locked them together with mounting urgency. Oblivious to all but their heightened senses, they were caught up in a web of sensuality.

But, even in the throes of her ardor, Hattie experienced a painful separateness, a mysterious chasm wedged between them, shattering the wholeness of union she so desperately sought. At the pinnacle of completion, it was she who held back, the totality of their union seemingly frustrated by cowardice or stubbornness. Some inner element, rankled, rose up, refused to submit. She was branded, ravaged by her own rebellious nature. He silently turned from her, unsettled, vaguely aware of the war being single-handedly waged against him. In some very basic primordial sense it was desecrating, yet impossible to touch on completely, its nature too elusive.

The next day they'd discovered the Marble Canyon Trading Post, a battered log ranch house fronted by a long, wooden porch with huge support posts. It was a general store—touting souvenirs, snacks, sporting goods, snapshots of triumphant anglers dangling their daily catch—housing a café in back.

They devoured what tasted like the best meal they'd ever eaten. So good, in fact, that they returned again several times over the next few days . . . .

Then she was forging down toward the destination they'd traveled hundreds of miles to reach, the basin of the canyon.

Her curiosity was assuaged by the sheer wonder of all she saw. A strange sense of lightheadedness came over her. She felt childlike, the same as she had as a young girl traipsing through her own private sanctuaries—Blackwater Creek, Dawson and Madden Parks of her hometown and the acreage known as Woodland not far south—secret retreats exuding dark mysteries, nourishing quietude.

In spite of a slight weariness in her limbs, she rarely stopped to rest, wanting instead to continue exploring the newness bombarding her.

During the last two miles, she felt at times like dropping, but, aware, the end was near, pressed on. She saw a bridge ahead spanning the Colorado. She stumbled down the narrow trail, reaching the canyon's lowest level to cross it. On the way, where Murdoch had stopped to rest, waiting to walk into camp with her, they noticed a plaque beside the trail marking the spot where Powell had landed after coming down the Colorado, the first white man to travel its length. Murdoch was interested in that more than anything on the trek. For him the historical significance was enormous. She felt his enthusiasm as he imagined the primitive, wild, isolated and completely natural territory as it must have looked to Powell when he first sighted it.

They walked the last quarter mile together, crossing the river into camp and claiming one small section of their campsite. Dropping off their gear they scampered around erecting the igloo-style tent to escape the clammy drizzle.

Rations were sparse because of weight limits, so they ate simply, mostly packaged dried meals, one of which they added water to, heating it up to eat before Murdoch wandered off to explore the fishing potential.

After lunch they strolled along the trail leading past the main string of campsites. A uniformed ranger, walking in their direction, halted as Murdoch queried him on fishing regulations, weather conditions, game department requirements. The ranger, easygoing, patient, accommodating, obviously used to similar inquiries, and Murdoch launched into an exchange of information and experiences including Murdoch's most recent at Lee's Ferry. To his amazement, after describing the strange thing he'd hooked into there, the ranger, from the description, determined that it had probably been a rare fish called the Humpback Chubb. Excitedly, Murdoch and Hattie glanced at each other as though it were some sort of omen of good things to come.

The trail meandered through a densely wooded area, twisting past campsites, rest areas, the ranger station, small shake-roofed cabins. After washing, they came back to camp where Murdoch gathered up his fishing gear, pulled on his waders, layers of socks, tackle vest, rubber boots and took off for the river, with Hattie tagging behind, eager to be by the river again. Its roaring, thunderously crashing sound thrilled her to a level of intensity she'd rarely experienced before. Her whole being vibrated, chilled and shivering, elated as she stood mesmerized by the river's surging force. It was as if it were beckoning her, as if she were so completely swallowed up in its essence that she would be cast out onto the crest of its current. It had a potently magical effect on her, and feeling wild and freed, she let all her inhibitions be swept away.

She watched Murdoch from a mass of rocks overlooking the river. He was knee-deep in water, fly rod extended, lost in concentration, causing her to feel alone, yet strangely peaceful, in harmony with her surroundings. The surging river, rugged boulders, spotty clumps of trees standing guard all vied to comfort her, calming her spirit, gravely offering friendship and solace, momentarily dissipating the heaviness weighted inside her.

Suddenly he turned toward her, holding her eyes, compelling her gaze to follow where he was pointing behind her. Together, in silence, they watched the sun set, visible through a deep cleavage between two massive canyon ridges. The clear, intense, indigo blue created a stunningly bold backdrop, causing her to gasp, staggered by the impact of such exquisite beauty.

In sharing that dramatic moment, a special bond seemed to grow between them, as if they'd witnessed some secret ceremony magnetically drawing her closer to him, closer, almost than any previous time they'd spent together. That night they wandered along a moonlit trail, crossing the river by a wooden bridge toward the old inn known as Phantom Ranch. Hattie, her imagination piqued by its legend, was intensely curious to see it. Discovering much about it was difficult, its form obscured by darkness. Interior lights shone from the entranceway and windows. Stepping inside, they found themselves in a large, well-lighted, cafeteria-like room laden with long, wooden tables, around which were seated a handful of late night diners obviously enjoying generous portions of homemade soup. Unable to see more without traipsing through the room in the midst of the meal in progress and having no reservations, they cut their inspection short. She had hoped to learn more, but retreated with Murdoch back out into the drizzle.

That night in camp, snuggled in their tent, Murdoch puffed contentedly away on his pipe by the light of a kerosene lamp that dangled from the rafters. Periodically he would pull out a bag of Sail tobacco, poking and packing it into the pipe's bowl. They'd dined on pan-fried trout, the day's catch. Together, in silence, they traced the glittering formations overhead.

The next few days Murdoch blissfully immersed himself in stalking the elusive trout, occasionally capturing one, then letting it go. She was absorbed in the battle between the man and his quarry, and in discovering the river, its rhythm, its grandeur. She would walk or sit for hours along its edge, memorizing shapes, colors, textures, not content just to see, but needing to touch, trace surfaces, classify, feeling the impact at work upon her, so strange and powerful.

They wandered over to the main cookout center, a covered three-sided stone structure containing a large grill pit. Several small groups huddled together to conserve body heat. Murdoch and Hattie, while heating tins of food, shared experiences with them. One pair had come from Boston, stopping there, before going on to California. A trio, two men and a woman, had teamed up in the canyon, two coming from New Zealand, one from Denmark. She was startled to realize that they were in the midst of a cultural melting pot, a priority stopover during first visits to the country. Murdoch, surprisingly, chatted amiably with everyone, while Hattie, more aloof, held herself slightly apart. She was not accustomed to an easy rapport with strangers, yet was fascinated by the diverse backgrounds and destinations.

On their last day Murdoch marched down to the river, on the side opposite his previous haunt, stealthily moving over the huge coral boulders lining the shore. She, impatient to begin the steep incline ahead, knowing the return would be slower and more taxing, started up alone. Over her shoulder she caught sight of Murdoch, his figure gradually diminishing. With little effort he could overtake her no matter how much of a head start she managed.

A blizzard was hurtling into Indian Garden, the overnight stop, when she stumbled into camp, soaked and shivering. Several people were huddled under an overhang seeking shelter from the gusting wind and rain. It was the apex of the same gale they had left behind at the top rim. Since the way back was several miles longer than the descent, Murdoch and Hattie had decided to divide it in half, allowing two days, with this respite in between. Hattie liked the spot. In better weather it would have been a wooded Mecca, complete with mountain stream curling through its center. She joined the others under the narrow eave, barely shielding her from the cold. She sipped a cup of coffee someone handed her. As she looked up, Murdoch was coming toward them from the trail, wearing only short pants and tee-shirt, his face ruddy-colored from the biting cold, grinning, oblivious to any discomfort his bare knees or exposed arms might be feeling. He came toward them, reaching greedily for the coffee handed him. He recounted his trip up, how he caught and released some good size fish, quitting in the downpour to run almost all the way back, resting only long enough to change his rain soaked jeans and shirt for dry clothes. She'd already chosen the campsite, roped off from the one next to it. It was on a slight incline but away from the camp's center insuring some privacy and quiet. She'd set the bulk of her gear on the picnic table bench to indicate occupancy. When Murdoch arrived, the tent strapped to his back, they set up a semblance of shelter. The night still stormy, she stifled hilarity as she and Murdoch, who groaned despairingly, watched a rivulet of water trickling across the tent's floor directly under his bed mat.

The next day they climbed out of the canyon finding, instead of the storm, a clear, brisk day. After dropping their supplies at the car, they headed for the venerable old lodge perched atop the canyon rim. Inside, she roamed through the main rooms, fascinated by the oversized scale of everything. The huge stone fireplace opening was almost large enough to accommodate her standing figure. Another climber who'd joined her on her trek up from Indian Garden, Murdoch already far in front, followed them in their search for something warm and strong. The lounge had a dark, cozy ambience that she responded to. She was relieved to sit and ease her aching muscles.

They ordered hot buttered rums ruminating all the while about their shared adventure. As the toddy seared through her, unraveling the knots of her weary limbs, a satisfied languor spread over her. She had done it, she thought, the knowledge inducing a strong feeling of pride. She'd done what she'd set out to do. The sense of accomplish-ment caused a lump of emotion to rise in her throat.

Murdoch seemed equally pleased with their expedition. He seemed to be more relaxed than ever since they'd met. He talked and joked with their companion while Hattie silently studied him, speculating all the while on his sudden joviality. He was a surprising plethora of nuances—a complex of caprices and enigmas, somber than shining—and some driving force propelled her on to reach the heart of his essence. In the mountain passes on the way home, he wove skillfully among the sluggish crowd through the slush and snow. After she commended him, he told her of the years he drove almost daily to the mountains to his ski patrol job, where he spent all his free time skiing on his own. He scaled the mountains, too, for rock climbs, fishing trips. He had no fear of mountains. At one with them, they were a part of him.

Murdoch was a man of few words. But, like an animal sharpens one sense to compensate for another's loss, he honed his powers of perception. She felt his eyes probe her in the dark. She sensed he saw her as the ideal of all the fragmented women of his fantasies. Many of her qualities seemed to amuse and delight, and to his chagrin, often vex as well. In the midst of her barrage of questions, he remembered the determined look on her face as she'd tackled the canyon. More student than athlete, she'd met it head on, undeterred, no small feat for her, he knew, posing a grave challenge, even risk. Her enthusiasm though less than zealous, astounded and pleased him. She was a fighter, met every dare undaunted that he proffered. He imagined her a raw jewel—complex, enigmatic, bewitching—luring him the master cutter.

As they drew closer to home, the terrain grew more familiar as they drove southeastward, past bulging produce fields. Near dusk they opted to camp in an open field for the night, huddling like two gypsy carpetbaggers in the sleeping bag in their car.

Their last day on the road was gloriously sunny, magnifying the scenic bounty bordering the North Cascade Highway, the billowy cedars, hemlocks, pines dancing in the breeze. As they crossed the floating bridge connecting the suburbs across Lake Wallington with the city, suddenly the oasis of Sealth rose up to greet them like a shimmering mirage.

Home again they spent the next days charging depleted energies, then took up where they'd left off before the expedition.

Hattie hurtled headlong into work on the room closest to her heart. She'd vaguely visualized the house both as home and studio from the first. It was time for the basement's transformation into an island of calm on which to fertilize her artistic juices, to paint, draw, excavate her dreams.

The floor was finished. Unused pipes were next, interim walls knocked out, moldy ceiling board ripped off. The initial aura of claustrophobia was purged, opening up into one vast L-shaped space. A new window replaced a warped, sagging door. But, her ideal began to materialize when a forty foot wall along one side of the room was faced with board, then wall where she envisioned material tacked, surfaces primed for culling her imaginings' creations into being.

New wiring, outlets and spotlights went in. Only the final stage remained. Paint and pan in hand, she set to work whitewashing the walls, ceiling, even the floor, to brighten the dinginess. It became a therapeutic rite for exorcising her pent-up furies.

Painting provided her starving spirit spiritual solitude—offered a realm for driven inner forces to flourish, spew forth with selfless abandon and emerge as the forms of her art.

Whitewash over hundreds of square feet rendered a startlingly fresh face, lending an air of purity, of stillness. She experienced a deep sense of security, serenity and peace as she began work in her newly created sanctuary.

She buried herself in her work virtually blotting out all else around her. She worked in a passion of burning fervor, the silence her only companion, drawing on a cache of elemental sources of her intrinsically primitive nature. The paintings began taking on a life of their own, emerging as from a chrysalis, variegated versions of some higher, idealized visionary world.

She was in the studio working every day almost before the paint had dried on the walls. She tore raw canvas off the rolls, stapling pieces directly to the wall, unstretched, blank, ungainly. Those vacant squares were unnerving, often causing pangs of anxiety to grip her. Some days she stared, immobilized, into the vast, white surfaces, incapable of moving her tools to action. Mesmerized by their very blankness, she sought to will inspired images to come forth, to dredge up the dormant mysteries of her psyche. And on rare days they came. Rapidly, flowing, tumbling one over the other they stumbled before her, astonishing and exhilarating her, flooding her with an inexplicable ecstasy. When in the midst of an idea she worked continuously, never stopping, nor wanting to, at times working for twelve hours at a stretch.

On good days she experienced a feeling of inner peace that eluded her more often than not. It was the sense of having achieved a productive day coupled with the evolving work in progress that buoyed her spirits. It was the essential vehicle of reaching into the center of her inner core, of nurturing her soul. Those hours spent in the private world of creation were her nourishment, the food she thrived on for existence, for survival. They furnished a direct path to her true being, to the recesses of her separate self. Every hour committed to her work reinforced the dedication enveloping her. She felt a slave, a vehicle for the creative urges welling inside her, using her body as a channel of release.

Murdoch disappeared for long stretches, suddenly showing at the studio door, seemingly craving her company. She sensed his resentment, resented his intrusion, his silent urgings that she give her energies and attentions to him, to the pressing needs weighing on him at the moment. Her commitment to her art was his rival, with him summoning all his wiles to draw her to him. The tug of wills began again. Unpremeditatedly, she had substituted her work for the disappointment and disillusionment of emotional entanglements. The threat of abandonment, of unfulfilled expectations were tempered beside the reality and constancy of her creative labors. Unconsciously she rebuffed his attentions, handing the burden of denial to him. The act of creation had emerged as her one Grand Passion, the passion she had coveted a lifetime, her one enduring love.

She desired above all a strong, secure, lasting, passionate connection of involvement but all previous experiences had died hard, frustrated, devastating, painful deaths ending in an annihilating abyss. She was frightened, Murdoch was frightened to begin again, to commit to a love that might not last. In some obscure way, they wanted proof of staying power, a fail safe policy warding off failure.

He came toward her, reaching out for her. She backed away, grappling with the tumult her churning emotions were thrown into by his sudden entrance. She resented his apparent indifference for her feelings, railing at the presumption with which he inter-rupted her work, treating it as if it were of no consequence.

Yet beneath the bristling mantle of pain, ran a shiver of pleasure, a delight in seeing his sunny face again, in detecting in those warm, pleading eyes the intensity of his need.

He was behind her, circling her with his arms. She turned to meet his lips with her kiss, pulling him to her as they slumped together in a heap toward the ground. All the caged, lonely, passionate longing came hurtling from her and he met it, boldly.

"Hattie," he whispered, "we're going to have to do something about all this passion."

Slowly, they mounted the stairs to her room.

Toward summer's end her persistent idea of going to the rainforest finally took shape. They decided to drive over. Their reasons for going were of a dual nature, hers to draw creative input from its mystery and poetic beauty, Murdoch to explore and fish its several rivers.

A Northwest native, she'd always planned on going to the rainforest but hadn't yet been. The Osprey National Park boasted at least three. It was nestled west on the fist-shaped Osprey Peninsula jutting into the Pacific.

First they stumbled onto the Hoq River rainforest embedded at the base of Mt. Orpheus. They were like wild children romping with delight through their newfound wilderness frontier. A rustic log cabin housing an information center caught their fancy. They wandered in. Colored slides of the forest's wild flowers, birds, animals and fish sparkled like jewels against lighted panels. Camping, hiking and fishing maps hung everywhere. Vacant staring heads, mounted and stuffed, glassily greeted them on all sides. Murdoch, in his element, purred with contentment. Years ago he'd scaled the summit of the mountain looming just beyond the door.

A velvety carpet of moss specked with tiny wild flowers cushioned the house. Narrow dirt paths led mysteriously into the adjacent thickets of underbrush and dense woodland. Silence, save for the lone cry of an invisible bird and a secretive aura hung suspended in the still atmosphere. Magical, it took hold of her senses, filling her with heady languor.

Murdoch learned from rangers that the best fishing in the Hoq River was upstream about sixteen miles. Learning this they decided rather to head south to the Kwinawt. It, too, was engulfed by rainforest. Forging through the thick underbrush, they reached the river rushing noisily along. River rocks along the shore made rapid travel rough. Instead she dawdled among the mass of strikingly marked specimens dotting the vast outdoor lab.

Murdoch scorned her interests, impatient to find a promising spot to wade into the river. Her loitering drew warning glares from him, urging her to step up the pace. River rocks didn't concern him at the moment, but defiantly she continued collecting unusual ones, and stuffed them into her pack to inspect later.

Up ahead, Murdoch delved into the current, settling in the middle of a shadowed pool close to shore. She entertained herself by busily rummaging further in the rocks. Just as Murdoch trudged back to shore, a torrent of rain ambushed them, sending them racing for cover under tufts of brush. Thoroughly soaked, they waited until the storm let up, then headed back to the van.

The next stop, they agreed, should be the Bodashell to the southwest. They entered down a steep dirt trail. Shimmering at the foot in an elegant array of richly wooded vegetation lay the rainforest, the epitome of all her imaginings. Suddenly she was Alice after eating the small cookie, or Dorothy in Oz; Guineviere in Camelot; little Mary in the secret garden. She was a bit of each of them at once, all of them combined and yet in the midst of a unique personal experience as though this were her own private woods explored for the first time.

A profound stillness infiltrated the awesome assortment of plant life flourishing in the dense woods around her, flooding her with peace.

Single file, they walked the path leading them deeper and deeper into the forest. Gray-green veils of Spanish moss draped huge arching branches infusing them with a mysterious, faintly tropical air. Every known species of fern lay in crowded clumps on all fronts, stretching ragged arms out as if vying for more space. Strange, exotic mushrooms poked up from the strangulating threat of clinging underbrush. One prolific fungus family sported broad, curvy heads dressed in white and pancake flat.

A thousand different shades of green spread out around them, a sumptuous wildlife smorgasbord. Her sharpened senses scaled to heights she had reached only rarely. The atmosphere emanated the distinctly pungent essence of the wilderness. Her limbs were giddy, intoxicated with anticipation and curiosity. For the first time in her life, she felt a wholeness that comes from feeling intensely and fully alive.

Huge ferns, lichen, alders, pines and massive hemlocks hovered as they trooped along the mossy, needle-strewn path toward the river. After trudging at length up small hills, down loamy cliffs and crossing over several narrow creeks by way of corrugated steel tunnels, they finally came into a rocky clearing, breaking into a trot, anxious to be at the river at last.

She had a sudden urge to strip and jump into the water. Only Murdoch's glare, sensing her intent, held her back. He warned her about the swift current and dangerously deep pools hidden among the rocks as though she were an unruly tot. Their eyes and wills clashed like flashing swords although grudgingly she admitted there was a kernel of truth in what he said. Sullenly, she plunked down in a heap on the rocks, feeling fretful and grumpy.

Grimly, she smiled with relief at her compliance when later, as a tiny Murdoch casted in the distance, two strangers clomped out of the woods, greedy for a forage in the river. Before long, disenchanted with their chosen spot, they lumbered off.

All the ingredients needed to induce euphoria were there. The silence, save for the sound of rushing water, the wooded surrounds, the midday heat warming her flesh. Yet the sun's rays couldn't seem to penetrate her inner chill. She could only slump dejectedly along the shore feeling utterly alone in the wilderness of her own despair. An unshakable shiver overtook her. She felt untouched and untouchable.

In the grip of an unfathomable malaise, she had an inkling of their numbing plight. They were irreparably, permanently, at odds. They were subtly fighting one against the other, secretly battling valiantly to retain a semblance of their two separate selves. Their desire to merge completely being so strong, it threatened to swallow them whole. They were unwilling to hand themselves up unselfishly one to the other, yet not satisfied with anything short of total mutual surrender.

She recoiled in horror recounting the innumerable acts of abject selfishness Murdoch had perpetrated against her. All the absences, silences, denials and refusals. The insatiable demands.

It has been said that pride is the enemy of love but without pride there can be no will and without will one can do nothing.

A creature of ample pride, Hattie understood then, as she skirted along the river's edge, its vast destructive forces. They were powerless in its grip. And yet, in the face of the unacknowledged war raging between them, Murdoch meant more to her than any other man she'd known. She responded to him in a way she never had before. She wanted him above all others. She wanted him to belong to her exclusively, to see only her, to need, want, love only her. But she knew that when the object of such an ultimatum was a man like Murdoch all efforts were futile.

In the midst of her sojourn to the rainforest a vision kept recurring in her mind—the small cabin would be snuggled among the trees, privacy from outside interference insured by the totality of its isolation. The imaginary structure would be of logs. The stone fireplace and chimney would be of river rock. It would be protected by woods, with a river or stream running through the property. Of weathered wood, the covered porch would be enclosed by a log rail. It would be near enough to the ocean to hear the roar of the surf, her spirit's salve. The house would sit in a wild, moor-like meadow of high reed grass, wild flowers, ferns, with a plat for cultivating a vegetable garden. Every inch of land would have an untamed, fresh abundance. Silence would suffuse the place. Her horse would graze in the pasture, returning to the weathered gray barn for oats and barley—a strong, solid animal, chestnut-brown with black mane and tail, its coat gleaming in the morning sun.

She would groom it, saddle it for an early morning ride along the beach before starting work in her studio, a shed between the house and barn. A private paradise to nourish her soul's creative spirit . . . .

Murdoch's quest, similar in content, encompassed a different arena. Returning to Southeast Alaska, his lifeblood, almost every year, he was growing increasingly caught up in its spell. He desired little else. It had drawn and nurtured him through seven summers. They talked at cross-purposes when describing their separate callings—hers to the coast, his to the southeastern edge of the far north. Her heart's dream spun around the sea and trees, his, the great rivers of Alaska.

Could they ever live together harmoniously or were they destined to remain apart, unable to reach a common meeting ground? Their future remained a mystery. Yet she was determined to pursue her ideal, to realize her dream, find the place embedded in her mind. She was sure it would appear at the perfect moment and she would be there.

Murdoch's rented house was up for sale, selling within the month. The only privacy accorded him was a tiny room on the first floor, smaller than his former one in the house he had first shared with his burgeoning family. Burgeoning, she mused, because soon after they met he casually announced his estranged wife was going to have another baby. First shock, then pain gripped her causing a knot of anger and disbelief to clench in the pit of her stomach as if she'd been slugged. Feeling helpless, despair rendered her chillingly withdrawn. But first she yelled "No!" in a sudden reflex of outrage. She felt not only humiliated but the victim of a malicious psychological plundering. All her positive, flowing energies toward him suddenly were sapped from her. Her face turned ashen as Murdoch sheepishly assessed his words' effects. He heard her groan, saw her deathly pallor. She felt the blood draining to her toes. He saw the devastation his verbal blow had dealt. Her limbs felt leaden, her spirit lifeless. Even though only knowing each other briefly, they'd bonded quickly. Then in a single instant, it was severed. She felt alone again, alienated from their initial melding. She realized their separateness and his deep-seated need to remain so. It was as though he were testing her tenacity in the wake of his crucial news. Overtly his demeanor registered him taking no responsibility for any wrongdoing. He considered the situation simply circumstances beyond his control, unpremeditated, unplanned. His wife had conceived some six months earlier in the midst of their separation, during a momentary lapse, in a feeble effort to reconcile. To Hattie, it sounded more like the woman's calculated conniving, in a last try at detaining him, or, knowing he was lost to her, affecting to hold a part of him through the product of his seed. In her sinking state of dejection the disgusting experience reeked to Hattie of abject manipulation, a deliberate plot to seduce him at the peak of her most fertile time. The entire episode sickened and disgusted her. She was anxious only to be far away from him, to purge herself of his selfishness and sordid milieu. She wanted to cleanse her soul, to recapture her freedom of spirit. She went away to be alone again . . . .

Hattie Ambrose had begun life in Odessa. The small, country town lay in the midst of a pastoral valley in the Northwest. She had attended the local public schools there—its grade school, junior high and high school.

All her free time as a young girl was spent running wild and free, like a spirited, long-limbed filly. Classroom hours served only to instill in her a curious pent-up feeling, her skittishness escalating daily. Hours spent at the small wooden desks assigned her over the years droned by, rarely piquing her rabid curiosity and fanciful imagination. From the first she was drawn to books, and relishing the few she found at home, had taught herself to read at the age of five.

She loved reading aloud to the class, sensing she had a clear, pleasing reading voice, exerting enormous efforts, when chosen to lead each sentence into the next, to pronounce each word correctly. The stories' banality didn't matter at the time. She was reading to the teacher and her classmates, had their undivided attention, the words flowing rhythmically, with the fewest possible pauses. She read constantly outside of class exploring magical, secret worlds previously unknown to her. She luxuriated in those distant lands full of adventure, fragrance and color. They never failed to quiet the vague gnawing within her.

The woods supplied the antidote for her increasingly jangled nerves. Madden Park, straight up the hill from her house on Worthington Avenue, was easy to reach. Up Birch Street, she would cross York, threading her way up through the field grass to the thicket's entrance. The poultice of its cool green spirit calmed the raw, open sore of her soul. In her private den, she savored its kaleidoscopic magic—clusters of mushrooms, unraveling fern shoots, campfire coals, the streak of a soaring goldfinch or bluejay. She never tired of the scene, wandering with a keenly honed sense of arousal, drawing each fresh discovery into her essence like a magnet. Dusk. The time all the giant firs, pines, spruce and hemlocks cast an aura of mystery, charging the stillness with wild expectancy.

Wilderness enchantment, wrapping Hattie like a soft mist, touched and deeply moved her fermenting core.

Daily tensions and nagging doubts fled in relief every hour spent in the secret port, an eye in the storm of her inner life.

One afternoon, Matt Dakota entered her woods like a stealthy young buck. Like a silent Indian scout, he climbed her hill, along the trampled path and into the heart of the woods, already, at midday, as dark as dusk. An eerie gloom shrouded them in ethereal, shadowy luminosity. He strode up ahead, intimate with every inch of terrain. He was the intruder, interloping in her territory. She felt fiercely protective and possessive toward her own. He sensed her resistance and understood.

As they explored the edge of a steep bluff, thunder crescendoed around them, through the valley below, bouncing off the canyon walls, deafening their surprised cries. No trees stood on that part of the bluff. As lightning flashed through the darkening sky, the frantic girl ran for cover in the wide open space. She heard a tree limb crack, break and fall somewhere in the distance. Spotting a trough, she headed for it, slumped in its crest and rolled into its cushioned protection. Warm rain fell over her, dampening her body and clothes until she was soaked. Glancing up, she saw a blinding flash illuminate the sky, sending a thrill of frightened excitement through her limbs. Then he was groping near her, swiftly covering her body with his own, trying to protect her from the impending danger. Her body was crushed deeper into the grassy bunker by the sudden weight of his, making her gasp and squirm at the onslaught. His breath warm on her neck, his head burrowing into her shoulder, his body's steamy warmth quieted her shivering. A foreign sensation gripped her, strange yet not unpleasant. Instinctively she grasped his neck, drawing comfort from his strength. Their gangly child-arms caught and entwined in a clumsy first embrace.

Their eyes held briefly like two surprised, wild animals, then looked away in confused embarrassment. Slowly releasing each other as the storm subsided, they rose silently and moved apart, the spell temporarily broken.

They descended the hill, going their separate ways. But the moment stuck in her mind, recurring often to haunt her dreams.

One day as she was hunting and gathering wildflowers, he appeared again. She watched him come toward her down the needle-strewn path overhung with broad pine boughs. He looked larger than she remembered. His dark, closely cropped hair formed a fringe over his high forehead. His wide nose ended in a slight beak at the tip. His full lips were red-tinged and fleshy. His muscular body was a compact medium-tall. He wore a faded plaid shirt and jeans. His steel-blue eyes crinkled when he smiled, spreading a web over his upper cheeks.

They knelt together searching for flowers. Totally concentrated on their new venture, they held up specimens for mutual inspection.

They rarely spoke. The slightest sound, intensified by the hush suffusing them, created an unwelcome disturbance. They communicated through natural instincts and sensory vibrations more than with words. The silence breaching them was bridged by meshing their sharply honed senses, a system of primitive instincts similar to that found in the hierarchy of the natural world. It was a complex of fleeting glances and subtle moves, signaling or touch. Verbiage became obsolete in their rarefied kingdom of intense feelings and imaginings. They reveled in unveiling mysteries leading them away from the mundanities threatening daily to drown them.

The woods supplanted school and homes, becoming both classroom and refuge. Life in the wild let their minds and bodies experience liberties they'd never known.

Once, in order to explore the territory around Blackwater Creek, they borrowed horses stabled at the farm topping Terra Cotta Hill. After saddling up, they headed out of the gray, weathered barn, over an open field to the woods. The horses, unprodded and steady footed, led them through the underbrush into the brooding forest. Ferns, moss, fallen logs, matted pine needles and leaves carpeted the ground, a comforting spread of wildlife. They were in their natural arena, where they could lower all defenses, exhale all tensions, breathe in the fresh, wild beauty with ease. The horses their sole companions, the woods their sanctuary, they forged into its heart.

The uneven grade through often rock-strewn terrain sorely tested the horses' prowess. The girl sometimes found herself pitching forward as her horse stumbled, suddenly railing at her tightened grip. Steep inclines prompted a dissonant melange of snorts and wheezes. Muscles bulged and rippled as they grappled with surprise obstacles. Glistening sweatily, they grunted and puffed along, nervously swatting and twitching their tails. With each downward plunge, the saddles creaked and groaned beneath the riders' bulk.

At last they reached a large, grassy clearing along the upper rim of Blackwater Creek where they dismounted, letting the horses graze and rest. Tying them to tree trunks, they went the rest of the way on foot. Slowly they descended into the depths, savoring glimpses of farms and pastures in the valley beyond.

They were content just being together in a comfortable melding of like spirits. They shared more time than with their own families. Inseparable, their bond soon grew beyond the woods, overlapping other days, though they didn't dare reveal too intimate an alliance at school. But everyone suspected. It was obvious, in their eyes, bodies and voices. They went to movies, dances and ballgames, walked and played together. It wasn't a physical union. Rather then being lovers, they were bound together as soul-mates Sexuality was anathema to their undeveloped emotions, as yet an unknown, dark, mysterious element lurking deep beneath their controlled exteriors . . . .

Matt Dakota was three years old when he came to town with his parents and younger sister. They had moved sixty miles north from a town almost identical to Odessa. Since his father was a logger, they moved often, following the company wherever it was doing forest reclamation, cutting or product development. He and Hattie were both ten when she first noticed him. She stalked him as one would a wild beast, tracked him down until she caught his attention, then withdrew. Slowly, his interest piqued, he took up the reins of pursuit, scarcely perceptible to anyone but Hattie. When his interest waned, she picked up the scent and took the lead, blazing the footprints of his trail. It became a mysterious hide and seek hunt, her one obsession. She yearned for him, to know him. And when he finally stood still long enough for her to approach, cautiously, he became her first real friend. She pursued him relentlessly like a hunting hound. Some days he came out of his house under the pretext of work to do and she was waiting. They stood together silently in the dark for hours, sometimes whispering. More than the cold air, her strange new discovery made her shiver with awe and wonder. He personified the dark, the forbidden, a powerful, unreachable presence.

He was solid, yet restrained, removed from any intimate connection. He seemed to prefer solitude, yet purposely sought her out. He was perplexing, infuriating, yet perpetually intriguing.

Matt Dakota posed an enigma to almost everyone who knew him. He rarely spoke and when he did it was in a low, gruff, halting monotone. His discomfiture around people infected others, making his self-consciousness painfully apparent. His eyes, heavy-lidded, jet-black coals, could mesmerize with piercing intensity.

He was an elusive solitary, more at home in the wild, wandering alone through the woods taking its still essence—fragrant, lyrical, tactile—to his heart.

Away from the woods, he floundered and shrank, as though the foreign atmosphere were too thin, of some alien element suffocating him.

Driven instinctively to the woods, wrapped in its organic womb, he sniffed and groveled, rolling like a fly-riddled horse to shake off extra debris. Burdened by a baffling malaise he moved woodenly further in, barely breathing at first, gaining strength as he went. Slowly the wilderness transfused vitality back into his body with its nourishing sap. His spirit replenished, he struggled to extinguish the cinders of discontent smoldering inside, fearful of being consumed by the dark terror.

Tests of stamina fascinated him. The more grueling the challenge, the greater his attraction. Second only to the woods, spectator sports fueled his spirit. He passionately embraced the demanding discipline and training of football. Every day after class he practiced on the field behind the school. Punishing warm-ups led to a barrage of running, passing and tackling until the game started. He pounded down the field exorcising the inner storm while waging battles along the way.

After months of working out, he began the season with teams arriving weekly for combat.

By game day, emotions heated, the air heaved with pent-up energy. The autumn haze shrouded the field in secrecy like an empty stage before curtain time. Finally the team charged onto the field, looking like a herd of angry bulls. The crowd, screaming and clapping insanely, thumped and chanted their impatience.

Matt, anxious too, paced the field like a caged bronco ready for action. Game days became a ritual of concentration and discipline. He ate little, took long walks in the hills to ease his nerves and taut muscles and plotted strategies. By game time his body, prepped and honed, responded to his slightest command. He was eager to play in the arena, the game and the uniform that suited his nature like a second skin. In action he adapted the same instincts garnered from the wild. He transposed into a stalking beast of prey, poised ready to spring on its hapless victim.

From the sidelines, Hattie felt a surge of adrenaline as she watched him skirmish with a brutish rival. She was repulsed by the bestiality yet aroused by the powerful virility.

The technicalities didn't interest her very much. It was the contest of wills, the battle of wits, the survival of the fittest that held her spellbound.

Matt Dakota's raging performance blazed and dazzled. Maneuvering slyly down the field he played not only on Hattie's emotions but carried most of the crowd with him. Foxlike, he wove among the bewildered defense, crossing triumphantly into the end zone holding arms and pigskin overhead.

His exertions were partly his way of courting Hattie in an athletically choreographed love-play to gain her attention and respect. On the field he was the star attraction, skillfully directing the action which usually revolved around him. In time his expertise matured dramatically, gradually overshadowing every other player. His became the singular figure to follow and Hattie, with the rest of his admirers, found herself falling under his spell. His body and movements were magnificent. His actions resembled a stunning ballet flawlessly executed.

Matt and Hattie still spent most of their spare time exploring the wilderness. Their friendship deepened into an easy camaraderie. He entered into manhood during their years together as she emerged from her childhood chrysalis, a gangly mass of long-limbed grace. At times they stared at one another as they would a stranger, their newly matured outer shells as surprising as freshly molted snakeskin. Both were filled with vague, unsettling sensations.

Hattie found solace in his company, helping to ease her discomfiture at home or in class. From her first day of school she suffered a debilitating shyness forcing her to escape into herself. The others found her aloof to the point of near arrogance. Staying to herself, she was tolerated but considered strange and ultimately dismissed.

Somehow different in her own mind and theirs, she became a castaway, separated by an invisible barrier. She was among, but not of them. They sensed in her a separateness neither defined nor understood. She seemed to float through their midst in a trance, oblivious to the indifference revolving around her. That it often degenerated into ridicule and scorn didn't concern her. She was in the private world she constructed as protection against her intolerable environment.

Delving into her lessons, she clung to them as though to a life raft, in spite of their mostly lifeless quality.

A new realm unfolded as she learned to write, the vehicle for broadening her crowded imaginary world. She loved forming letters, relishing the unique shape of each. Methodical, deliberate, she practiced pages of capital and small case letters for hours. One page of capitals, one of small, she combined the two sizes, each with its own way, feeling strangely attached to the whole array. They became her friends, a welcome means of expressing even her most convoluted thoughts, a detour around her clumsy tongue to reach further outside herself.

She stayed mostly to herself, except for one other friend besides Matt, in junior high school. A young girl the same age living nearby, and Hattie, played for hours together.

In the sandbox or playroom they transformed mounds of sand or piles of blocks into something tangible. Hattie, seduced by the creative act, exulted as roads, buildings, whole cities took the shapes of her ideas. Molding sand like wet clay she carved the houses, gardens, streets and castles of her fantasies into reality. Arranged domino-style, small pieces of wood became roadways, terraces, towns.

Once, they plundered her grandmother's steamer trunk, billowing in luxurious silks, satins, sequins, beads and brocade. Grabbing a black felt fedora, suede, open-toed high heels edged in gold sequins and wriggling into a slinky, sequined gown, Hattie emerged a fashionable woman of the world. She shed one outfit, then donned the next. Swimming in a blur of fuchsia, scarlet, lavender, violet, they strutted in successive guise, Egyptian queen, ethereal dancer, glamorous movie siren until they dropped, exhausted, onto the jumbled heap of castoffs.

She spent most of her time at home alone either reading or sketching. During those hours she felt the creative juices drain from her, seep away drop by drop and slowly evaporate. Some strange undercurrent stifled the air, a strangulating sadness that clung about the place, contaminating everything.

The gloom offended her highly tuned senses and her spirits plummeted. The red brick house had a steep Tudor-style roof and a high dormer window in front. A large picture window was to the right side of the front door and a row of smaller ones to the left. Giant rhododendrons partially obscured them, shutting out a good deal of light. Sitting on the corner, the house faced a busy street. Several hawthorn trees lined the parking strip along the adjacent street. The house, fairly large, had three bedrooms, a living room, dining room, den and three baths including the one in the basement. Its three stories soared menacingly over the driveway, tiny yard and narrow alley in back. Huge cedars and hemlocks sequestered the garden from street view. A small sandbox sat to one corner and seedy flowerbeds held clumps of wild, purple iris.

Off green dominated the living room. Twin mahogany bookcases, their insides a darker green, skirted the large windows at the far end of the room. They held porcelain vases, candy dishes and other sundries but few books. The room felt cold. The carpet, embossed with flat spiral swirls was beige. A scanty oasis of color centered on two armless coral chairs facing each other in front of the fireplace. Grotesque flowers blotted the long draperies in several shades of green against cream.

The dark dining room housed a massive mahogany buffet along one wall. Doors and moldings were deep, red-stained mahogany. The only window was swathed in mesh drapery.

Hattie spent most of her spare time in the den. The room was small and covered from floor to ceiling in mouse brown—the carpeting, walls and upholstery. Several narrow windows lined one wall but failed to lift the gloom. She devoured books by the hour, drew, colored. She sat engrossed in chilling mystery programs or music on the radio. Her mind and spirit yearned for knowledge and beauty.

She floated in her secret world behind a veil of silence. Acute shyness kept her from sharing it or her budding ambitions. Her mounting intellect and special interests seemed of little concern to the others. She was left to forage for her enlightenment's own fuel in order to keep its insatiable appetites supplied.

She was alone. She was lonely. There was no one with whom she could share the burden of her isolation. She wasn't close enough to her best friend to confide in her. Some days she could barely move. Her limbs were leaden with despair. She slept more than ever, taking long naps every day after school. Her spirit was slowly dying and the woods were its only hope of survival. She remembered walking through the woods with Matt and she wished they could share those times again. They alone might provide the solace and serenity for her soul. In a daze, she walked up through the high, scorched grass. Soon after starting, she felt the heaviness flow out of her limbs. After reaching the woods, she started down the path toward Terra Cotta Hill. She walked for hours in a semi-trance, plodding her way along the familiar trail. Occasionally she glanced up, startled by birdcalls or rustling leaves. Foraging on, she gradually felt her energy return and picked up the pace. Several miles later she came to the clearing and Hayden Farm beyond where riding horses were stabled and boarded.

Mrs. Hayden, a short, plump, middle-aged matron, sported a cap of salt and pepper speckled curls. Seeing Hattie, she bustled toward her full of good cheer. She was very generous with her horses, letting Hattie ride them anytime.

Together they led one of the old standbys to a hitching post fronting the grayed barn. Cora Hayden, a veteran horsewoman, had been breeding and racing horses with her husband since his retirement fifteen years earlier. She coddled and fawned over them as if they were children. They'd become her surrogate family with the departure of her own brood's fourth and final member.

Impeccably tended, their grooming, feeding, nursing and birthing were full-time rituals. Mrs. Hayden took great pride in her equestrian duties, considering them to be labors of love.

Placing blanket, then saddle on the mount's back she adroitly cinched and buckled the girth into place. Hattie held its nose while the bit was gently shoved between its teeth, harness pulled over its face and ears and reins laid across the saddle. After Hattie had mounted, Mrs. Hayden proceeded to tighten the stirrups to fit her legs.

She turned the horse toward the woods and slowly walked to the entrance. Its rhythmic gait along the path created a familiar, hypnotically constant sound.

Nothing but the horse's hooves hitting the ground disturbed the stillness. The subtle air of tranquility settled over her. She was in the woods again, the world she knew and loved more than any other. Her newly-awakened body unfolded, opening like a flower. Stretching her arms high and wide, she felt every muscle tauten in the struggle to relax.

Her movements became one with the horse. They melded together in synchronized unity, meshing more completely with the underbrush the further they penetrated into the wilderness. They rode on and on, maintaining a slow, steady gait, pressing further into the heart of the forest. About midway, between Terra Cotta Hill and the distant clearing, they came to the reservoir, down left from the hill. Hattie veered her horse toward it. The horse, suddenly uneasy, softly whinnied, snorted and tossed its head, straining away as she pulled in on the reins.

As they neared, she heard rustling from the reeds around it. Startled that she might not be alone, her eyes scanned the grounds for signs of an intruder.

Then she saw the stranger. He emerged from the tall grass, walking slowly toward the spring. Oblivious to Hattie's presence, he strode to the fence, grabbed hold of the edge, then, resting his chest over the backs of his hands stared broodingly into the water. Not glancing in Hattie's direction or acknowledging her in any way, he stood silently, completely immersed in thought.

His preoccupation allowed Hattie to observe him further. He was over six feet tall, extremely slender but well proportioned so that he didn't seem unusually thin. His striking profile revealed a prominent, aquiline nose and bold, jutting chin. His large head was exquisitely formed with a mass of sandy-blonde hair the color of ripe wheat. His hands were large with long, tapered fingers. He wore a buckskin jacket, plaid loggers shirt, jeans and leather cowboy boots.

Hattie dismounted, wrapped the reins around a tree and slowly approached the stranger. He stood rooted, calmly watching her. And when she looked into his eyes, their intensity pierced her like an arrow. A translucent, smoky gray-blue, they were deep and observant. Startled, she stepped back, swaying slightly off balance as if they had struck her. She bristled at his arrogant, almost possessive perusal. Yet some compelling force drew her to him.

They stared silently at each other for a long time, like two wild animals meeting for the first time. Each approached the other with guarded curiosity, nostrils quivering, sniffing the newcomer.

He was of a breed never known to her before, one of worldliness and mystery. His eyes held a sardonic gleam—wide, old, tinged with pain and suffering yet tender, kind, sly.

Her presence softened his rigidity. He relaxed his stiff hauteur, appeared approachable, less forbidding. He sensed her inquisitive nature. In a glance he saw before him a wild, free spirit; sensuous, sensitive, a solitary child-woman, both strong and vulnerable. She was tall with an unruly mass of chestnut hair flowing to her shoulders. Her long-limbed frame was delicately structured, almost gangly in its litheness. Her aristocratic stature struck him as that of a young thoroughbred, shy, skittish, poised for flight.

Then she was escaping. She fled to the spot her horse was contentedly grazing and mounted. Before he could stop her, she vanished into the forest, leaving him to muse on the mysterious stranger who'd so suddenly awakened his senses.

Then Hattie knew the stranger was Ram Canby.

He lived on a farm in the neighboring town of Chinook. His parents were dairy farmers, distributing milk, butter and cheese to the various wholesalers in and around the two towns. When not in school, he helped out around the farm, milking, crating, feeding and tending the herd. Any spare time he spent reading or playing his guitar.

Ram Canby was essentially a loner. He had only three close friends—two from school and one, a fellow band member. His two great passions were music and poetry. His life revolved around practicing and reading. Steinbeck was his hero. He devoured every word he'd written with awe and reverence. To him he was The Master. The great concern with the impoverished, downtrodden masses portrayed in Grapes of Wrath had moved and permanently altered him. His was a poetic, sensitive nature, camouflaged by haughty cynicism.

The Canby Farm covered nearly seven acres. It was reached by driving ten miles out the Old Thaxton Highway to Pioneer Market, a dilapidated country store and filling station. There one turned left onto North Fork Road, drove about half a mile to Macomber Road, then right just before reaching the bridge spanning the north fork of the Skyhecan River. Macomber Road skirted the upper edge of the Canby property. The ancient pines, hemlocks and elms lining both sides of the narrow, bumpy road, their arms arching overhead, blotted out the daylight. A quarter mile down Macomber, barely visible, a steep, rutty dirt road led down to the main drive.

The old farmhouse was built of split-logs piled one on top of the other over slabs of plaster. A saggy, weathered cedar porch, open except for the log corner posts, fronted the house and was reached by going up four rickety wood steps. Medium-sized, wood-framed windows faced a vegetable garden on one side, the porch in front, a large yard with fruit trees on the other and the river in back.

Ram spent most of his free time down by the river, playing his guitar, reading or writing poetry, exploring the river, dreaming.

There was a narrow, overgrown path off to one corner of the property that led down to his favorite place by the river. It was a section where the river elbowed, forming a large, still pool that everyone familiar with it called the old swimming hole. Further upstream to the left were some rapids and huge, old fallen logs spanning almost completely across the river causing more turbulence. From that corridor the river flowed downstream, around the bend where the still pool was and on down along the section below the Canby home, down toward the falls much further beyond.

The upstream corridor was lined on both sides with thickets of huge trees, tall reed grass, wildflowers and low-lying shrubs. The thick profusion of vegetation cast dark shadows over that section and the black hole at the far end, where the river came seemingly out of nowhere, lay sheathed in darkness, an endless tunnel leading to the unknown.

Ram went there, after first meeting Hattie, to sort through the powerful stirrings she'd aroused. He felt bewitched, in the grip of some magic spell magnetically propelling him toward her and completely helpless.

Her mystery besotted his mind. He knew nothing of her, not even her name, only that he had to see her again, had to find her, must know her. She embodied that elusive ideal he'd been searching for all his life. She moved with the grace of a jungle cat. Her copper hair glittered in the sunlight. Her lithe body was erect, with queenly regality. He'd been stunned when he looked into her eyes—soulful and glowing like fiery, bronzed amber. They had roamed over him coolly like a soothing caress, intense and candid, reaching into his core, searching out his essence. In those few moments, she'd captivated his spirit, taken part of his deepest self with her.

He walked slowly back to the house as if in a trance, went to his room, took his guitar down from the wall rack and began strumming softly.

His room, adjoining the large, open front room, was lined with cedar, its fir floor bare and scuffed. It was small and sparsely furnished with an old pine chest, nightstand, ladder back chair with a rush seat and a narrow wooden bed covered by a white, hand-crocheted spread. Grayish-white cotton curtains hung on either side of the high, small-paned windows looking out onto the vegetable garden and grazing pasture beyond. A huge hemlock just outside the corner of the house kept the room in perpetual shade.

Propped against the foot of the bed, he sat on the floor plucking his guitar. He was too preoccupied with thoughts of Hattie to concentrate on the music. Distant sounds came to him as if from a dark, fertile wooded place filled with glowing campfires, dancing, music.

His senses were stirred to new heights. His body, throbbing and reverberating with longing, metamorphosed into a maelstrom of long-suppressed passions which were surfacing, threatening to intrude upon his serenity. A profound yearning infused his deepest recesses causing his fingers to strum in intense, agitated strokes across the strings of his guitar over and over as if to call forth the apparition of his desire. He poured the contents of his soul into his playing as the exquisite strains, haunting and melancholy, suffused the room. His lovely melodies reflected the driving, tumultuous inner sensibilities seeking release, yet disturbingly inept at mitigating the gathering restlessness within. Some inexplicably powerful force compelled his movements, overwhelming his ability to contain the flood of heightened emotion.

Exhausted from grappling with his turbulent inner demons, he went out the kitchen door to the cobblestone terrace.

An old, weather-beaten picnic table, two long wooden benches and a cluster of mismatched chairs took up most of the space. Tufts of moss and grass in between the stones lent an air of wild abandon. Clay pots overflowed with tangled dried herbs and trailing grasses. Wooden baskets of wildflowers stood along its edges near the porch. A stack of firewood was piled near the door. Giant pines and hemlocks hovered just beyond the far edge casting shadows over the courtyard on one side and huge fanning branches leaned out over the river on the other.

It was the hour of dusk, the sun sinking behind the trees below a luminous indigo sky. The river became one long, undulating ribbon of ruffled purple shadows moving in serene elegance below the wooded bank.

Ram stood in silent homage to his favorite hour when the hushed calm over farm, woods and river seeped into his spirit.

He began plotting his next meeting with Hattie. He knew only that he must see her to still his inner tumult. Tomorrow, he decided, he would go to the woods again in the hope of finding her.

After school, chores finished, he set out on foot over the ten-mile stretch to Odessa, his long strides quickening with desire.

Not until he'd reached the hill rising into the forest did he stop to rest and calm his pounding, heaving chest. Winded, he had no intention of stopping long, even though his limbs and muscles felt stiff and strained. He lay down in the tall grass, panting and gazing up to the blinding white September sky.

After a short rest he continued on until he reached the woods. Immediately he felt the impact of its hushed darkness. The only sounds heard over leaves and twigs crunching underfoot were the songs of the birds.

Soon he came to the clearing where a large campfire pit lay surrounded by low iron bars and grating. Several rows of stones had been stacked around it and cemented as a barricade against the wind. A three-sided, shingle-roofed shelter, housing a wide, wood, built-in bench stood just behind it.

Flopping down, he leaned wearily against the planked wall, his head and neck arched back. He closed his eyes momentarily, trying to quiet the anguish raging through him.

Then he heard a horse clomping toward him. Startled out of his pensive retreat, he jerked up to see the same bold stare of the mysterious girl. Their eyes met and held suspended, breaching the chasm holding their bodies apart. Slowly, she lowered her gaze, releasing him from its paralyzing intensity. As if drawn by a magnet, she dismounted, holding the reins tightly with one hand as she started toward Ram, her horse close behind.

Then, wrapping the reins around a post, she sat down by Ram in the tiny alcove.

Without a word he drew her to him, pressing her body to him with a groan belying his outward composure. All the pent-up ardor was unleashed in the heat of their frenzied entwining. A flood of unloosed passion obliterated rational thought, urged them further, drove them deeper into the grip of its raging wake. Sniffing, smelling, each inhaled the other's fragrance, as if it were some intoxicating potion necessary for survival. Wildly, their hands and lips sought the source of their desire. Fingers grappled with buttons and belts, pulling and tugging to free their writhing bodies.

Suddenly Ram pulled her down with him to the soft dirt. Falling, rolling together hungrily, their mouths searched out an unending opulence of straining limbs. Lips burned, bit and bruised, impatient to devour and savor the swollen succulence.

Never taking his gaze from her passion-glazed eyes, he lithely mounted her soft, silken length, holding her arms to restrain their thrashing. Then with one surge he plunged, searching, probing, into the core of her mystery.

Their spirits floated upward and out, expanding, exultant as they strained to sustain the rhythmic harmony. Time was suspended. The inner music guiding their movements filled and rendered them oblivious to all but their shared ecstasy. Stretching out the slightest touch to prolong the union, each burrowed deeper into the other.

As if initiated into some secret society through a private rite, both believed they had taken possession of the other, while still retaining the individual essences of their single entities. They had delivered themselves unreservedly one unto the other, yet remained whole in the essential uniqueness of their beings. They had become one yet the strength and depth of the wellspring of their inner resources allowed them to hold sacred their separateness.

As Ram released Hattie, he rose to collect his loosened garments in chaotic disarray. He was, simultaneously, struggling to regain some semblance of order in the reigning turmoil of his still disheveled emotions. He moved as if in a state of shock, struck by the realization that the most intense, most private passages in the dark corridors of his being had been touched and stirred by the powerful forces moving within the girl.

Never had he experienced such overwhelming feelings. The power the girl wielded over him was unsettling. But, gratifying, too, knowing the intensity of their response to each other. They were twin spirits in pursuit of a deep, giving, total communion. And each, uniquely, relished the joy of fresh revelations. The rare heights they'd reached nourished and rejuvenated them both.

Languidly procrastinating, finally parting, Ram backtracked through the woods. Hattie, dropping her horse off at the Haydens retraced her way, then up to her family's new ranch house.

The move to Hillcrest Road came just before Hattie first met Ram Canby. Lofty-beamed, picture-windowed, the low, cedar sprawl faced out over the faintly discernible town below. And on clear days one could look out past the great valley to the massive mountain chain beyond.

Living on top of the hill symbolized arrival to the enterprising Ambroses. Plans had been in the works for several years. A carefully chosen city architect regularly barraged them with new sets of blueprints. With consternation, the Ambrose adults waded, stewed and swayed through each new batch, seemingly unable to agree on the final outcome. Tension ruled those days of plotting and construction. The points on which they disagreed seemed endless. To Hattie's delicate inner rhythm disruption was harrowing. She shriveled back into her shell, shunning, as much as possible, any further clamor. After a year of preparation and building, the Ambroses carted their voluminous headquarters to the near-vacuous shell.

Rambling over half an acre, its main floor touted vast areas of vaguely defined living space. Often divided by only a skeleton wall, one cell flanked another. Looking unfinished, the interior was purposely minimal. There were three small cubicles and a bath relegated to the children on the lower quarter. Their only distinguishing feature lay in a tiny patch of colored carpet.

Each had one picture window looking out on a smattering of vegetation, one closet and one set of wooden drawers. Nothing unusual differentiated one room from the other.

Hattie recalled a single day and evening at home with her family:

After spending the afternoon with Ram, she retreated to her room. She peeled off her coat and clopped down on the makeshift sleeping bag bed. Eyes closed, she conjured certain fleeting images, desperately trying to etch them indelibly in with the other characters and moments already crowding her mind.

A spontaneous rapport had sprung up between her and Ram. She'd never before known the intoxication effected by their natural melding.

She could still feel the pressure of his lips, the luminous penetration of his eyes, the strong, gentle roving of his hands. Together they had meshed into a ballet of sensuous, flowing lyricism. Again she let the strange, new sensations sweep through her in a fugue of muted aches. She shuddered from a flood of flexes and twitches as if in the throes of some heated delirium.

Freed from the suffocating vise of bitter longing, she floated and soared to her cloud world of exquisite peace and light. She focused exclusively on the recent phenomenon known as Ram Canby. All her other thoughts paled beside her vision of their union. Even Matt Dakota's shadow cast no more than a speck on her conscience.

She faded out of her fantasy as Mrs. Ambrose called sharply from the hall and, without waiting for a reply, burst into the room scowling in disapproval.

Ella Ambrose didn't indulge in, nor tolerate, idleness of any kind, especially daydreaming. Her days were partitioned off like an office interior. Sectioned into quarters, only the lunch hour was free for fortification and rest. Forty year old Mrs. Ambrose, exuding robust health and well being, was constantly bewildered by Hattie. She considered her two boys reluctantly manageable, but Hattie continued to baffle her, often causing her to feel outsmarted.

Theirs was a guarded affection pitted with misunderstanding, exasperation and impatience on Mrs. Ambrose's side, resentment, wounded pride and a dread of prying on Hattie's. Rather than risk confrontation, each actively avoided the other.

Her mother's eyes frisked her suspiciously, a silent question punctuating her accusatory perusal. Their eyes deadlocked. Mrs. Ambrose, noting Hattie's unreceptive mood, decided to broach her recent whereabouts later. Turning abruptly on her heel, she retreated. Hattie considered it a minor triumph and escaped back into her brooding. A vague heaviness settled over her, setting her adrift in a fitful sleep.

She woke at dinnertime. The only time of the day the whole family congregated, it was Hattie's hour of agony. Her frustration at having so few outlets for expression doubled in the din of the family's clamor.

Mrs. Ambrose always presided glumly at the head of the table, Mr. Ambrose precariously holding his own at the foot. An almost tangible tension threaded between them, emanating from Mrs. Ambrose like an unraveled spider web.

Her censorship of all controversial subjects lent an abstract air to the proceedings. Anyone who crossed the taboo line warranted her scathing disapproval.

James, the oldest sibling, always incurred her scowl of distaste first by embarking on some verboten topic.

Seventeen and a Westend High senior, he was gearing up for the Debate Club competition, feverishly weighing worthy subjects. Topping his list of contenders were capital punishment and capitalism.

Soon he launched into a heated monologue equating the power brokers of big business with the lowest form of life.

"The scale of equality in this country is overwhelmingly tipped in favor of the giant corporations and the upper rung of the economic ladder. The uneducated, downtrodden masses are being trampled into the ground by self-serving money grubbers and oppressed by power hungry corporate moguls."

At that point, James, red-faced and winded with self-righteous fury, slumped back in his chair while his parents exchanged stricken glances, especially Ella whose face was taut with consternation.

Donald, the second oldest, sullenly toppled a pile of uneaten peas, several scattering to the table and floor.

Hattie usually retreated into oblivion during one of James's diatribes. Her eyes glazed over with a faraway glint of insouciance. Her equilibrium shifted awkwardly to the present from her musings. The air was tropical with tension.

James's satisfaction at creating another stir never failed to dismay her. He thrived, in fact his life-blood depended, on controversy. Skipping slyly from face to face, he gloated inwardly at how successfully his outburst had shaken his audience out of its infuriating complacency. He was visibly gratified to have ruined one more evening meal.

Hattie long before had disposed with the idea of venturing forth any of her own ideas. It was something her ferocious pride wouldn't let her admit. She assumed an ascetic guise of mute profundity, using her eyes and gestures to convey her opinions. She was there in flesh but her heart and mind craved escape. Her own firm views were so anathema to James's that any challenge she might pose would have ended in warfare.

Mr. Ambrose, though possessing an almost poetic intelligence, remained attentively stoic during most nightly performances. His ability to listen, honed and perfected, had reached museum quality. His senses were acute but, like Hattie, he chose not to participate except for a periodic nod or shake of his formidable brow.

Pushing back his chair, he sometimes saw the red of an angry bull as he heard James's slant on politics and economics. Occasionally they butted heads or clanked horns in a deadlock of flaring eyes and nostrils.

Mr. Ambrose did little to revamp James's thinking. Figuring it a lost cause at that point, he left him to his wayward course, destined to run amok.

After doing the ritualistic table clearing and dishwashing, Hattie fled to her sanctum to finish her homework. She always rushed through it to delve into her own stash of romances, poetry and classics from the library. She devoured the flowing words like an elixir. They flooded her ravenous soul and spirit with nourishment.

Wordsworth. "Ode on Intimations of Immortality".

" . . . Though nothing can bring back the hour of splendor in the grass, of glory in the flowers, we will grieve not, rather find strength in what remains behind . . . ."

The words underscored an already impermanent quality hovering over her bonding with Ram Canby. She winced in pain and frustration, thinking of the evanescence of things.

Their recent beach outing unfolded in her mind's eye:

. . . She and Ram heading to the ocean, Ram at the wheel, Hattie scrunched in the middle beside Mrs. Canby, stiffly propped against the door on the passenger side.

Driving down the arrow straight shaft of Old Central, they could see so far along the stretch ahead that it looked like it shot right to the horizon and thirty-mile beach beside the Pacific.

Hattie, snuggled next to him for such a long time, left Ram feeling slightly unnerved. Distracted hugely from his driving task, his thoughts and glance rested more often on her than the road. Both felt enormously pleased with themselves to have forged the excursion into being. Ram pleaded tirelessly until his father finally agreed, warning him that the plan wouldn't materialize without a chaperone.

On the way, a new facet of his personality unveiled itself—Ram, the entertainer.

While stone-faced Mrs. Canby sat in complete ignorance, unable to see through Hattie, Ram contorted his face into absurd positions, forcing Hattie to hoot uncontrollably. His tongue, pushed to the limit of his right cheek, met Hattie's gaze with a prodigious mound of flesh protruding like a beached baby whale. Then the dagger tongue darted forward pushing his upper lip out until it curled out and under like the trunk of a drinking elephant. The lapping dog motions were followed by the tongue and top lip projecting out in slow synchronized rhythms like a crew team's oars. While Hattie squirmed uncomfortably in between outbursts, she felt the chaperone-statue stiffen further.

Her guilt at causing Maude Canby's discomfiture, and fearing she'd think them rude, cruel and laughing at her, kept Hattie from glancing in Ram's direction.

The nearer to the ocean they came, the more expectant and restless Hattie grew. Since childhood she'd felt the same impatience and excitement to arrive still made her fidget.

Racing pulse, thumping heart . . . tick-tock, tick-tock, tick-tock . . . with the steady beat of a wound metronome . . . tock-tock . . . tock-tock . . . like a resonant old grandfather clock. Her inner ear vibrated and crescendoed with sounds echoing the incoming tide.

Driving through the small coastal towns, familiar signs indicated they were almost there, charging her with even greater need to reach the sea. Rustic, weathered wood cottages in various stages of dilapidation lined the main streets. Some owners boldly displayed their family name carved into driftwood slabs jutting up from unruly grass.

Mostly the yards were enclosed by small wooden fences, some white picket, some of rough-hewn, unpainted cedar.

Beachcombers' loot hung from every rafter. From netted glass floats to the tiniest seashell, bric-a-brac was strewn over railings, steps, driftwood, window sills and picnic tables.

Fresh fish stands cropped up plastered with pictures of the day's catch—crab, oysters, clams, mussels, trout and salmon.

A familiar musk heavily perfumed the foggy salt air.

Rounding the Miranda cut-off, a string of darkly luminous mudflats emerged. Mirage-like, shining, still pools banded gently against long sandspits.

The closer they came to Gray Bar, their seaside destination, the larger the pools grew. Gradually all the tide flats expanded and merged until nothing but sea lay before them. Finally they got to Gray Bar.

The town was swarming. It was mid-August, high season for vacationers coming to the beach loaded with children, pets, bikes, cycles, boats and campers.

Rowdy teens, frantic for action, gunned motors, raced, honking and screeching through town trying to attract some enticing passerby.

The sun had just set. Night lights flooded from the shops, cafes, bars and amusement parks along main street, illuminating the wood planked sidewalks through open doors. The air circulated with congeniality. Amiable proprietors extended a slightly forced hospitality to the new batch of patrons, painfully aware that they carried the bulk of the annual income.

Ram drove Hattie and the shadowy Mrs. Canby through town at a turtle's pace giving them a good view of the carnival-like activities.

Near the heart of town he pulled onto the Beachcomber Motel's circular drive and stopped at the office.

The L-shaped chain of tiny, white-washed cabins, topped by red tile roofs, was the quintessential beach motel. Neither shabby nor elegant, it quietly offered modest comfort at a moderate price. The ocean was only two blocks away, its roar faintly heard from each cottage.

Ram swiftly paid the customary advance and was given the key. Going a short way they found their little niche, oddly distinguished by a bold-faced ALASKA painted over the door.

Scanning the other entrances, they discovered their home's curious nomenclature wasn't unique in its dubious distinction. Each one had been dubbed with the name of a western state.

Two steps and a small landing led to the somewhat dingy interior not easily differentiated from a thousand other beach cabins.

The main room was bare except for a chrome-legged Formica table, four folding chairs and a large brown sofa. The floor was covered by greenish-brown mottled linoleum. The miniscule kitchen housed a refrigerator, tiny sink and counter-top with two elements. Two small bedrooms separated by a bath were at the back of the cabin.

Mr. Canby-Martin to all who knew him—had stayed behind on business. He planned to join them for a few days, then drive home with his wife, giving Ram and Hattie more time together during the drive back.

Ram and Hattie, restless and cramped from the two hour drive, needed fresh air and left to explore the sights. Mrs. Canby, tired from the drive and strain of the stranger in her midst, pleaded a headache and retired early.

After dropping off their luggage, they drove to the nearest market, picked up some beer and headed back along Beach Street, still buzzing with cruising cars and strolling couples.

Famished, they wandered into the Surf, a brightly lit greasy-spoon. Settled amid gold-flecked, red vinyl, each scanned the menu. The usual assortment was listed along with a scanty selection of local dishes, though nothing more than coarsely battered, fried clumps of frozen fish.

Finally filled, they set out for the beach. Turning off Beach Street, Ram slowly inched his way along a darkened side road. Two blocks away, they came to the town landmark—a huge, crescent-shaped arch boldly stamped: GRAY BAR—THE WORLD'S LONGEST BEACH. Loose sand covered the road approaching what looked like the world's largest advertisement. Sitting looking beyond the enormous structure, Ram and Hattie stared through the blackness, barely able to discern the white caps of incoming waves and stars dazzling overhead.

The car cautiously crawled down the long, sandy promenade to the beach, directly ahead. Gradually they descended to the ocean's edge where Ram veered onto the dark stretch of hardened wet sand.

Windows open wide, night air blustering through their car and hair, Ram and Hattie shrieked happily at their newfound freedom.

They drove mile after mile, reveling in the spaciousness, solitude and peace surrounding them.

After what seemed like an eternity to Hattie, Ram slowed to a halt, came around to her side and pulled her playfully toward him from the car.

They had to shout to be heard over the sound of breaking waves.

Skirmishing like wild beasts, they yanked each other in an impromptu tug-of-war dance perfect for performing on a moonlit beach. They ran, scrambled and chased until the air felt chilled in their lungs and their sides ached. Flopping down on the cool sand, they lay side by side, winded and panting, gazing up at the stars.

All at once Ram rolled over next to Hattie, as near as he'd wanted to be since they'd left home.

Stillness fell over them like a soft veil. Moonlight lay on Hattie's face, illuminating it with such a radiant glow that Ram held his breath for fear of disturbing the vision. He'd never seen anything more exquisite, nor magical. A lyrical grace infused their limbs. The soaring magic between them spun a filmy golden web over their bodies, entwining them like delicate threads of exotic carpet.

They fused together with the uninhibited deliberation of swimmers under water. Slowly their unreined desire overflowed, spreading ripples of raw sensuality through them. A luminous sheen of moonlight played hide and seek on their nakedness, molding, from the chiaroscuro of curves and valleys, two polished marble statues.

Throughout the driving, plunging possession, Ram knew a surge of passion and unity with Hattie more completely than he'd ever thought possible.

Gradually their shaken senses stabilized. Parting reluctantly, they realized their merging spirits had risen to a rare and exalted kingdom.

Suddenly Hattie jumped up and started running down the beach with Ram in hot pursuit. They ran and ran, the steady thud of their legs and feet pounding the sand, faintly echoing the thunderous rhythm of the waves.

Charging, gulping the salty night air, hair and clothes flying, Hattie fled along the sea, her path forged by the moonlight. Flailing like an ethereal sea bird taking flight, her arms waved and fluttered as if she were soaring up into the inky space before her.

Finally, winded, she fell face down onto the cool sand, stretching her arms and legs out as far as they would go, grasping the earth in a passionate embrace.

Then Ram was there, exhausted, damp with exertion, collapsing to the ground beside her. Somewhat mystified by her impulsive departure, he gently gathered her to him, holding her closely, protectively as if anticipating another sudden departure. Slowly, he quieted her, caressing her soothingly, stroking her hair back from her face. Warm lips whispered against her ear, hypnotically, guiding her consciousness into complete relaxation until they both descended into a deep, trance-like sleep.

When they woke, it was very late. Sure that Mrs. Canby would be anxious, they knew they'd better get back to the cabin, fast.

Fully alert and exhilarated with tension, they hurried toward the solitary shadow huddled on the beach ahead.

Ram jumped in and started the engine, which in its neglected state, finally responded garrulously. Fierce with impatience, he pounded up and down on the accelerator forcing sharp, grinding noises from the clutch and changing gears.

The rear wheels treaded frantically, spinning with the zipper-like sound of a zither. He urged the sluggish beast back and forth, again and again, gripping the wheel as if the sheer strength of his will might move them forward. The back end sank lower, the wheels dug deeper until sand almost totally obscured them.

As Ram groaned and muttered, Hattie could only stare, trying without much success to stifle a mounting urge to cry.

Rapidly assessing their plight as temporarily hopeless, Ram climbed out, vanishing in the dark to find some help.

Trotting back along the sand-road strip and under the looming sign, he found a gas station blocks away still open.

A small, red tow-truck sat idly to one side. The driver lolled benignly inside the tiny, glass office, pouring over a paper while munching a sandwich.

Hearing Ram's tale of woe, he readily agreed to come to the rescue. On the way to the beach, the driver chatted easily, clearly well-versed in the aged ritual waged between man and sea.

Finally freed, Ram and Hattie barreled back to the cottage and, motioning shushing signals to each other, tiptoed to the front door. It was locked. Momentarily panic-stricken, they skirted the house until Ram tried opening the bathroom window. It was grudgingly stiff, creaking stubbornly. Ram went first. Hoisting his body up over the ledge, he was half in, half out when Hattie, unable to suppress it any longer, started giggling hysterically. Choking, muffled laugh sounds came from Ram's upside down half. Righting himself, he grabbed Hattie's hand clamped tightly over her mouth and yanked her toward the window. Following his lead, she slithered over the sill, into the tiny dark room, nearly knocking herself out on the sink.

Catching each other red-handed, so disheveled, full of the feverish mischief of naughty children, further tempted them to howl. Only Mrs. Canby's loud coughing and squeaking bed sobered them into silence.

After a long, parting kiss, they went their separate ways, Ram to the big brown sofa, Hattie to the tiny back bedroom.

Martin Canby arrived the next morning while Ram and Hattie were still asleep. Ram awakened to kettles clanking over the low murmuring of his parents.

By the time he was fully awake and came to greet them, he knew from his father's face and voice that he'd already received some vague impressions of the previous evenings' events. Mr. Canby, a strict disciplinarian and somber by nature, was not amused and scowled disapprovingly at Ram. It was soon apparent that the reunion was not off to a very propitious start.

When Hattie finally stumbled into the kitchen she found the grizzly form of Mr. Canby seated behind his intent scrutiny. She'd only met him once or twice when she and Ram stopped at the farm to pick something up. She silently endured his rude gaze. She wasn't used to being visually dissected and found the experience demeaning. Her head went up and, holding herself erect and proud, she locked eyes with his, feeling more timorous than her outward poise conveyed. She wasn't certain but thought she detected a slight admonishment, a warning signal to settle down and act more responsibly. Later she suspected the chastisement may have been self-imposed by her incessant conscience. Ruthlessly conversant, it sometimes weighed her down like an overbearing monitor. She stood her ground and Mr. Canby's glance and haughty demeanor retreated back into some invisible shell behind the barrier of his gold-rimmed glasses. She rarely saw him again so she was never sure what she'd seen on that benign countenance except that it contained a certain remoteness and haunting melancholy.

They all spent the rest of the day down at the beach, walking, futilely attempting to dig out a burrowing clam, wading and hurdling shallow waves. Sporadically Hattie felt an odd, yearning twinge somewhat familiar, but of mysterious origin and significance. That same inner tugging, like ropes being twisted and pulled, gripped her as she lumbered along with Ram. She had a sudden yen to rip off all her clothes and plunge into the ocean. The deep sparkling blue lured her into its fathomless leagues. Intoxicating, exquisite, nothing less than total immersion in its forbidden essence would satisfy her. It might be an experience of the same magnitude as the devastation wrought in a tornado's wake. On seeing the limitless lapis-lazuli blue, bejeweled and glimmering, she was stunned into silence by its breathtaking beauty.

The musky sea scent made her so dizzy that she nearly fainted from giddiness. Warm ocean mist wrapped her in a delicate web and spun her like a reeling top.

But, more than tricks the rarefied air played on her senses, was its subtle way of lifting her to a loftier place. By glimpsing infinity she rose to the brink of grasping elusive, eternal mysteries. She began to juxtapose herself against the scope and context of the universal whole. Briefly she staggered upon that chamber of enlightenment leading her to see the infinitesimal speck she made. She was suddenly oppressed by a sense of futile, hopeless insignificance. But, on another level, she was almost euphoric to feel in step with her surroundings.

Deep inside she clung to a tiny slice of light dragging her from a sense of doom to one of harmony with the universe.

Ram's silence gave Hattie's thoughts free rein. They dipped and soared in sync with the seagulls, then fell into a soliloquy of their own:

What is our purpose? What do we seek? Do we belong and if so, how? When will the sadness leave, when can we breathe? Why are hearts so heavy, eyes full of tears, limbs nearly numb? Existence. What does it mean? Happiness. What is it, who finds it? Fulfillment. Who will know it? Peace. Harmony. Truth. Honesty. Goodness. Wisdom. Will they come and in what form? To live on as many levels as possible—is this the path to wholeness of body, mind and spirit. And love—most important, elusive and difficult—is it the ultimate quest . . . ?

What increasingly bothered Hattie was the widening distance between her and Ram. Sometimes, when together and he was especially attentive, she felt lonelier than when by herself. Ram, though physically there, dwelt on mysterious matters remote from present reality. He often was so still and pensive that she forgot he was with her. He rarely spoke, yet for brief, exquisite moments, they communed exclusively through their senses in deep, rich symbology. Later she surmised he'd probably been preoccupied with future plans too unformulated to share. Eventually she learned Ram Canby was a man with ambitious dreams. But, unaware of them at the time, Hattie knew only that he found her presence vital and escalated their time together. It never occurred to her to thwart his musings. She cherished contemplation as much as he. But when the need arose to disclose secrets, hopes, desires, they were sadly inept at expressing them. Their increasing verbal inadequacies and indifference began to pall on Hattie, compelling her to either improve the situation or abandon it altogether.

Thinking back, she tried to recapture exquisite moments she and Ram shared as an antidote to her collapsing personal world.

She recalled another time with Ram, standing alone, propped against a far wall listening to music. It was Friday night and the place was crammed with dancers and musicians. The dimly-lit haven from prying parents' eyes was known to locals as the Zorro Club.

Ram and Hattie came in separate groups of friends. Hattie remembered how he'd looked:

Standing there so erect and proud he had the chiseled form of a noble Greek god—an Apollo or Adonis.

His mop of straw-colored hair stood out in the dim light:

His hair glows as if lit by a thousand fireflies.

Impeccably groomed, he wore pale blue over a white shirt and tan slacks. He was clean, crisp and easy-going. His bemused, observant aloofness intrigued Hattie, drawing her to him. She boldly met his challenge by asking him to dance before he could escape. They moved as if welded together, their limbs meshing as from the same mold. He moved with the same rhythmic beat as in a ceremonial dance. For once, Hattie felt she belonged, that she was shielded from danger behind the protective barrier of Ram's towering figure.

The clubroom, atop a scale of rickety steps, housed the huge, scuffed floor, wall of cloudy windows and bits and pieces of lumpy furniture.

Band members and their equipment filled the low platform at one end around the corner from the concession stand.

The room, that night, had been packed with dancers, musicians and drop-ins. Stomping feet and thudding music shook the walls. Unable to talk over the din, Hattie floated through the background drone, soothed by its steady beat.

She and Ram held each other tightly, barely moving on the dance floor, afraid to disturb the mood. Having finally found a safe port, nothing could disengage them.

Later they met the others at Barney's drive-in, but hardly noticed them. They guarded their secret with furtive glances smoldering with desire.

Impatient for privacy, Hattie wondered when they could spend more time together. Ram, too, was restless to be alone with her, even if only for stolen moments in some secluded park or backwoods road. Sometimes, at her house, they had peace, but their best solitude was while driving country roads, rarely speaking, but still communing deeply.

They knew almost all the back roads around the two towns by heart, happily content exploring them. Rustic farms, fields, mysterious woods and winding rivers entwined with their senses to nurture their thirsty souls.

But that night, after the dance, Ram drove Hattie up the hill to her house, according them a rare chance for privacy.

Those exquisitely simple moments Hattie had cherished most. Though somewhat taken for granted at the time, they were gentle and tender, appreciated even as young as they were.

They stretched out their time together as long as possible before Ram had to get back to the farm. She still saw him standing by the back door, canvassing her face for a spark of interest. Evidently he found one, because he swept her to him and his kiss felt as natural as breathing. Everything about him was subtle and unassuming. They held each other for a long time until Hattie stirred uncomfortably and pulled away. They were somewhat awkward and tentative but sincere and, finally, after a long, scorching silence, they parted.

In her room again, Hattie reconstructed the evening. Ram Canby was quickly pressing into her world and she was trying to sort out her feelings about it.

They'd just met so she wasn't sure yet if she harbored any unbridled passion or secret love. But she was gratified to have found such a warm, trusting friend.

In light of their intensifying bond, she warned herself to proceed with caution. Having suffered through the loneliness, emptiness and disappointment with Matt Dakota, she resolved to avoid becoming embroiled in anything remotely like it again. She would preserve her own identity, dreams and goals in spite of Ram Canby.

And Ram was discovering, to his surprise, his growing need for Hattie. Rather than threatened he felt decidedly buoyed by their deepening involvement. Although his first emotional or physical tie, he knew it was serious, that she embodied the ideal he'd pursued all his life. He was slightly bewildered by the sudden onslaught of feeling, as waves of delirium washed over him. He felt somewhat cowed by the strong, new sensations, yet deeply moved.

He knew that he was irrevocably in love with the shy, intense, young woman. He also knew she'd wielded a spell over him, entangling him in her magic web. He was glad she didn't seem aware of her supernatural powers.

Hattie, alone in her room, sadly concluded that she'd never had a real friend to believe in or confide her heart's innermost secrets. Every single person had slowly shattered her delusions of trust, leaving her lost and despairing. Ram was no exception. He, too, had started to wither her expectations. Somehow he was withholding his deepest self, unable or unwilling to share his feelings, further alienating her and rendering her more of a solitary than before they met. Her craving for intimacy and need to belong escalated until she felt she was drowning in her pent-up passions. She was a pawn in the grip of some monstrous force she could no longer control.

It was the kind of sensation she knew from her darkest dreams, like falling fathomless depths into the unknown.

Her dreams were more often frequenting her daily experience, merging her unconscious existence with her waking reality. She vividly recalled her latest fantasy. The previous night she'd slept fitfully, immersed in an obscure vision, bizarre yet lifelike.

She dreamt she'd been a guest in some baronial mansion. Exactly where she wasn't sure, only that its rooms and layout seemed vaguely familiar. Some kind of celebration was in progress. The guests icily acknowledged her. Her persona watched helplessly as the macabre drama unfolded.

She'd already forgotten some parts of it, but fragments recurred. Horribly maimed faces, unrecognizable yet distinctly human, haunted her. She remembered most clearly roaming from room to room meeting the aged, hairless ghouls. Without acknowledging her, they sent her on to the next room where she found even more hideous creatures. Finally she stumbled into the last room. Everything was completely obscured from view, but she stood in the doorway trying to make out what was going on. A shaft of light disclosed something flickering wildly in the dark. Just as she was about to turn and bolt away, a shiny saber blade came crashing down and decapitated the vague object before her. She'd awakened from those haunting visions damp, exhausted and bewildered.

Since meeting Ram Canby the unsettling excursions occurred with ritualistic regularity, disturbing her normal balance.

She withdrew from the chaos connected with Ram, seeking solace in other diversions. She'd brightened up her usual school day gloom by signing up for the art class.

During that particular hour she felt slightly revived by the quasi-creative atmosphere. For one meager hour, a parsimonious beacon amid the general pall of stagnation, she lost herself in sketching, designing and painting. Oblivious to all but her own creation, she allowed her instincts free rein. Her imagination, gathering momentum, soared above the buzz around her. Her only twinge of anxiety arrived with the instructor each day.

Mr. Brighton, medium-tall and slightly built, wore enormous opaque-lensed, tortoise-rimmed glasses. He sidled into class and immediately inhibited all proceedings. The sardonic set of his tightly-pinched mouth suggested a disdain for his tedious charges. The tiny dark blots obscured behind thick, milky glass, pierced with an ironic glint. His wiry, weasel-body moved stiffly in its armor of haughty superciliousness. It was less than golden for the students outside his select realm. Hattie, not one of the chosen, was always uncomfortable and often humiliated by his pointed barbs. In retaliation, she drew on a determined concentration to thwart his invasion of her domain. She was left alone with her work whenever she could rally the strength.

Something was always happening in the art room. Sets for the school play were built, posters silk-screened, pottery kiln-fired, murals painted and program designs were printed.

But, Hattie, heedless of the bustle, found it a jeweled sanctuary shimmering along the stony drudgery of the other hours.

Losing herself in designing a reverse pattern of black and white forms, she was startled to hear Mr. Brighton's softly taunting voice overhead.

"And what have we here, Miss Ambrose? Are those intended to be rolling pins or bowling pins? It's probably just as well that I can barely make them out among all the clutter around you. How can you work in such conditions?" And with one last churlish grin, he was gone.

Deflated and shaking, Hattie knocked over the India ink bottle, the ink spilling over scattered papers and dripping onto the floor.

Mr. Brighton cast an even wider grin back over his shoulder.

She never saw Ram during the school day. He went to Chinook High five miles west of the Canby farm. But he called almost every day after school and they'd talk and laugh for hours. Some days, when he wasn't practicing his music or studying and she was free from seeing friends or school projects, he'd come in to see her and they'd drive over back roads to be alone.

But they were drifting further apart. Ram was seeing someone else. Hattie was shattered, and, when she learned her rival's identity, incensed. Two years behind her at West End High, Georgiana Hacket was red-headed, promiscuous and completely unscrupulous. Hattie had believed the love between her and Ram inviolable until he'd sensed her misgivings and slow withdrawal. Her doubts triggered and fueled his own about her commitment. The breach, unconsciously bred by Hattie, gradually widened to admit strangers, decompressing their intensely intimate sphere so that Hattie no longer sought refuge in it. She'd mistakenly thought theirs was an unwritten code of exclusivity with territorial rights. The advent of Georgiana brought the ultimate demise. Her heart felt permanently mutilated.

Georgiana was a mere diversion for Ram, a poultice for the festering wounds of his rumpled pride. His fragmented nature hovered between possessiveness and vulnerability. Of exquisite sensitivity, its roots grew from deeply embedded distrust and an unforgiving streak that was irrevocable once stirred.

The ensuing days and nights dragged endlessly on for Hattie. She withdrew, casting Ram completely out of her thoughts as if he'd never existed. And for her, he no longer did. She was inconsolable, refusing to accept his attempts to reconcile.

It was several months before she could stand his presence. Their tentative reunion was extremely uncomfortable for her. Ram was placating, trying to draw her out of her shell of renunciation. He came to her, hesitant and humble, dreading that he may have severed the only real communion he'd ever known.

They headed into the darkness toward town in order to have some privacy.

Odessa's two-block-long main street held the bank, two insurance agencies, jewelry store, drugstore, clothing shops and hardware store, in addition to assorted bars and restaurants. The San Modisto Hotel stood on the corner in antiquated splendor, regally overseeing the operation of daily commerce on the sleepy country streets. The Fort Café sat to one side of its swinging glass doors. Hattie and Ram pulled up in front of it and went inside, slid into one of the vacant booths and ordered sodas. At that late hour, the large, open, brightly-lit room was nearly empty. They sipped their drinks in an almost deafening silence.

They drove along old Central to Nisqually State Park and turned in at the gate to the loose-graveled parking lot. A wood bridge crossed the river running through the center of the grounds. At the center of the bridge they leaned close together, draping the railing facing west. Moonlight filtering through the giant hemlocks dappled the water with the festive air of strewn confetti and streamers.

That was the moment Ram broached the foremost subject on his mind since discovering Hattie, the woman he thought he'd never find.

Pulling her close, nudging against her fragrant, windswept mane, he felt more fulfilled than ever before, more potently aware of the directions and meaning of his life and that she was the embodiment of his boyhood dreams and ideals brought to fruition.

"Hattie," he whispered, "I've been doing a lot of thinking about the future and what I want to do. I've decided to become a lawyer, specializing in labor law."

There was a long pause made longer by the dense stillness.

Hattie didn't answer. She knew nothing about the law. No one had ever mentioned to her anything about it. The only time she'd heard it discussed was when her parents' long-time friend, attorney Clyde Barston and his wife, Emma, came to visit. It always sounded like a very vaulted, mysterious realm from which she felt remote and vaguely excluded. When Hattie didn't answer he went on, "I want us to be able to be together like this forever. I want us to be married."

The silence went on until it seemed as if it would deafen them. Still Hattie didn't answer.

There, Ram thought, I've finally said it, finally gotten it out—what I've been wanting to say since the first time we met.

He was so relieved having told her his plans and feelings for her that he didn't realize until just then that she hadn't answered.

The silence roared.

Finally her voice, a tiny defenseless sound in the vast woods, came as from a very long distance.

She was still reverberating from the shock waves his revelation had caused. She hadn't realized that he'd been considering anything permanent. She'd assumed they would go to college, probably different ones and gradually drift apart, probably never seeing each other again. But then Ram was telling her he wanted to spend the rest of his life with her, see each other every day, have a family together, love each other *forever, feel loving toward each other every day for the rest of our lives.*

She was too stunned to reply. Her mouth, dry and tongue-tied, wasn't moving right, didn't do or say what her mind told it.

Finally her mind and voice connected in a small, halting, foreign sound. It was a trifle rushed as if she could hardly wait to finish saying it.

"But Ram," it sounded a little winded, "I can't get married for a long time. I have to finish college before I can even *start* thinking about marriage."

There. It's out in the open. Those impulsively spilled sounds were cast into the wind, free agents of devastation, never to be forgotten by either of them and never to be retracted.

Neither of them spoke during the long drive back to Odessa.

But nothing was ever the same between us again.

Hattie left for college, thinking there would be plenty of time for a deeper understanding to develop between them.

Her error was to assume anything about Ram. She completely misjudged his temperament, impatience and vindictive streak, forgetting her tendency to expect more, always seeking some unknown quantity just beyond her reach.

Thinking back, signs of estrangement were there long before the final break:

The pool in the garden the night of my sixteenth birthday shimmered in the moonlight like an exquisite jewel. I'd greatly anticipated that day, knowing it was one more step to independence. The swimming party that night brought expectant friends to help me celebrate.

Ram came in the afternoon to help with the last mad dash to get ready. But when I dropped the bottle on my foot and cut it, I had to go to emergency for stitches. Ram was beside me all the time, full of concern.

On what was supposed to be one of the best days of my life, I sat in the midst of the revelry, watching from the sidelines while Ram stood by in grudging attendance. It was a miserable night. Feeling dejected, I brushed him away, treating him like a fly to be swatted off. Catching my mood like a contagious disease, he drifted off early.

And the occasion of her brother's sudden marriage:

James had gone east to college, bringing his best-man back for the wedding. I was instantly enthralled.

Carl Jensen, dashing and blonde, loomed larger than life, all magic, mystery, sophisticated charm.

In one fell swoop, he personified every romantic hero I'd ever read about. He made me feel like a dazzling butterfly fresh from the cocoon whenever I was near him. He exuded charisma, a magnetic pull I'd never known and could only try to analyze later.

But for those magic days of his whirlwind visit he shone brilliantly with the finesse of a veteran actor, strutting briefly before his adoring audience.

Catching me off guard, oblivious to my vulnerability, he gorged himself on my banquet of awe. One final round of bravado before bouncing merrily off, an elusive genie, a puff of smoke, dissolving back into the shadow land from whence he'd come.

And through it all stood Ram, steadfast, another captivated, if disgruntled, member of the audience. His presence had been obliterated by the shadow of Carl's dramatic shuffle.

He grew exasperated with my infatuation, drank himself into a stupor on wine punch, then stormed out. Drunk and distraught, instead of driving home he passed out, huddling and shivering, in his car. When I found him in the morning, ragged and rumpled as if he'd spent the night in the depths of hell, he felt strong enough to move. But before I could reach him he left in a cloud of dust, spewing flying debris in his wake.

They both went to the state university but lost touch. He sought solace in a young woman's arms, a misplaced soul like himself, in the grip of some shattering calamity. Wisps of details about him filtered down to Hattie from her Odessa friend going to the same college.

The doomed young woman carrying Ram's child knew of his past, that he didn't love her and was finally driven to suicide. She would have died if Ram hadn't found her near-comatose body. Ram's father thought it his son's duty to marry her. They were inextricably bound and eventually married. Hattie felt like she'd been in a bad dream strewn with all the elements of a tragic play, a comedy of errors, each detail fraught with more pathos and incredulity than the one before. It dogged her college years, dragged her along as if she were weighted down by a ball and chain, deadening her spirit so that she moved like a sleepwalker and no one ever suspected the origin of her leaden malaise.

Sleep became her best friend, blotting out many daylight hours and all of the nights.

The psychic pain interrupted her studies that faltered and flagged, often coming close to a standstill. She never fully joined in the activities or lives of the people around her, maintaining an aloof, shadowy distance caused partly by timidity but, more often, sheer indifference. Nothing around her seemed to rise to any level of significance.

She felt like she'd already lived through several lifetimes with nothing fresh to discover, no more pain to endure.

To outsiders she moved with the self-possession of a worldly woman though she was only a child lost and bereft, grieving for some intangible . . . .

Then, from her reverie, Hattie's attention was jarred back to the present by a bulky figure huddled over a large canvas on a spindly wooden easel.

Suddenly reminded, by the unfamiliar surrounds, that she must be miles from her seaside sojourn's starting point, she focused on the scene before her. She stopped below a sprawling, old manor house with badly peeling whitewash, weathered eaves and sagging shutters. A narrow path overrun with clumps of tangled dune grass led from the beach to the house, which sat in solitude beyond a tiny forest thick with pine and birch.

Hattie glanced back to the strange, intently absorbed figure. She saw that her own form was his object of interest and was being just as closely scrutinized as his canvas. The easel, its legs plunged into the sand, stood against the vast backdrop of silver-blue sea. Turning from it, he watched her, bearing the same noble grace, dignity and assured strength of the bronze or marble figures of the ancient world. Slowly she strolled toward him, along the edge of the sea, as if it had been destined.

At close range, the full intensity of his deep, gray gaze scanned her like radar. His features and manner revealed little. She couldn't detect anything personal, resorting instead to carefully perusing his physique.

Bearlike, he stood much taller than she. His full face had as its centerpiece a hawklike beak, with the flaring nostrils of an aroused bull.

His broad, square-tipped hands spread an enormous span. A tuft of wiry hair, slightly red-tinged, like a walrus's overhung his upper lip, almost obscuring it from view. The fleshy lower one protruded in a permanent pout.

Everything about him seemed over scale. He exuded an air of expansiveness, of wide-open spaces, of secret, mysterious, monumental places.

His hair, his least distinctive aspect, being of no particular color other than medium-brown, was somewhat sparse on top, not bald or even balding, just spare-looking when compared to the vast expanse of brow and forehead below.

Wide shoulders joined the broad chest that ran straight down without any indentation at the waist, all of which were attached to long, stocky, trunklike legs.

All of these parts, when pieced together, comprised a face, a figure that were less dashing or handsome than imposing and intriguing and, to Hattie, very mysterious.

Rex Dravus, well-known and respected Sealth painter, tenant of the old Grandview cottage for several months, thought the woman sauntering to him the epitome of all the graceful loveliness and wild beauty of a young Daphne. Like the ageless wood nymph, her haughty bearing and spirited demeanor seemed curiously poised for flight. As she neared, she took on all the classical beauty of an ancient mythological goddess. She embodied the essence of all that was supremely, sublimely, exquisitely beautiful, becoming beauty incarnate.

As they stared at each other like baffled children, an almost tangible electric current passed between them.

To avoid the first awkward moments, Hattie glanced rapidly at the large canvas. She was immediately struck by its pervasive somber alienation. Somewhat unnerved, she felt slightly chilled, yet also more deeply aware of the devastating isolation of solitude.

The exuberant brush strokes and magnanimous composition, devoid of constricting boundaries, didn't lessen the melancholy underscored by the soft, subtle palette. Nor did their taunting playfulness, cajoling one to come and frolic, suggest anything lighthearted.

Though imbued with magically lyrical, poetic passages, it wasn't particularly endearing. It didn't embrace the beholder, didn't unequivocally compel one into its mysterious universe. But it did, circuitously, provoke one to spend awhile meandering through its complex grandeur. Most startling were its aspirations of genius. Still, Hattie retained her initial reserve, somewhat disturbed by its dual nature. She detected a vague hauteur underlying the general tone's strained rigidity. But it piqued her desire to discover and dissect more of his work.

She felt him surveying her. She turned to look at him, but he'd pulled a shade over his features, making it impossible for her to read his thoughts. He stood stalwart, his great arms crossed against his chest, his legs spread in a Paul Bunyanesque stance.

Sensing her interest in his work, he invited her to the house and studio next to it that he'd converted from a barn. Indian-style, they headed up the path to the screen door in back.

Hattie found herself in the midst of a huge light-filled aerie. Windows lined two whole walls of the huge kitchen. Terra-cotta tiles covered the long, narrow, rectangular floor. In the center sat a colossal harvest table strewn with newspapers, baskets, dried fruit, assorted art materials, spice jars, cooking utensils, herbs and grasses. The great porcelain sink faced toward a section of grounds that covered nearly twelve acres, spreading down to the beach. Part of the studio shed could be seen off to the left.

Through the dark, wainscoted hall, they came to the largest living room Hattie had ever seen. She imagined it similar to that of some baronial European estate.

A massive flagstone fireplace dominated one wall. Large enough to hold a standing figure, it was surrounded by a white-washed brick mantle and slate hearth. Mammoth bronze andirons sat inside the vacant open structure.

The vast dark wood floor was splashed with variously patterned Oriental rugs of brilliant colors.

The snow-white walls and ceiling reflected the cloud-sheathed blanket of sky pouring in through the windows and glassed-in front door, rendering the room blindingly light. Over-scale antiques, a curious blend of Gothic and Baroque, sparsely outfitted the space.

Hattie and the stranger climbed the broad, turned-railing steps left of the fireplace to the top floor.

Ribboned down the center by an Oriental runner, the long upstairs hallway was flanked by several small guestrooms, a slightly larger master bedroom and two baths with antique fixtures and patterned ceramic tiles. It, too, was light-filled. From one bedroom window Hattie looked out over the grassy backyard, past the trail leading through the trees, shrubs and dune grass, to the breaking waves and endless sea beyond. For her the scene cast a spell of magical enchantment. The sight of the sea never failed to thrill her, made her shiver, filling her with delight, peace, at sharing such majesty.

Going downstairs again, Rex led her beyond the living room to the rambling veranda, a Victorian relic snugly abutting the southern exposure. From its antiquated splendor, Hattie, looking down its length between the two western corner columns and over the trees skirting the lawn, caught her breath as she sighted again the wide-open sea.

They walked past the kitchen to the double doors of the studio.

Inside, a magical spell fell like a net over Hattie. The space seemed draped in filmy muslin by light filtered down from hundreds of tiny, glass, ceiling panes veiling it in exquisite stillness.

Every wall was lined with canvases propped facing in. Scattered down the middle were various workbenches, stools, chairs and a large, wooden easel holding the work in progress. Some of the visible canvases stirred Hattie, moving her almost to hysteria.

Some elusive force compelled her into their idyll of earthly delights, the entire body luring her into a lush paradise of haunting woodlands.

Her spirit's deepest, secret part soared up into flights of fancy.

As she and Rex silently circled the studio, she paused before every painting and, as if by command, he turned it around for her inspection. Many were still only seedlings, but in each a living entity was germinating. And, finding one finished or near completion, the impact of its lyric force caused Hattie to swoon.

Suddenly aware of the painter, the treasures' perpetrator, she felt her cloak of self-consciousness descend again, steeping her in an aloof rigidity, unceremoniously bringing her back to the present.

Charcoal drawings worked directly from while painting papered the walls. They served as studies for determining areas of depth and distinguishing shaded sections from highlighted ones. And as she glanced from a drawing to its painted counterpart, she saw the skillfully applied technique in operation, how a variety of pigment values were subtly, yet lucidly, graduated, separated onto several different planes and, in the process, drew the eye into the painting's heart.

She saw the masterful care with which each painting's surface was prepared, the terra-cotta oil wash mixed and used on both wood and canvas for an undercoating ground as another means of achieving depth and luminosity.

In fact many of his skills and techniques paralleled those she was developing in her own work, only more advanced. She, too, used a ruddy earth color ground utilized by the Old Masters of the Renaissance. She, too, was struggling with problems of depth, luminosity and value gradations. But more than with the technical dilemmas, she was grappling to decode emerging mysteries not only of the external world but those from deep within herself. Her paints were intimately linked to both her vision of universal mysteries and mysteries of the human psyche. Her paintings focused heavily on timeless universality but also celebrated her personal relationship with the world.

Experiencing Rex Dravus's world on his professional turf, she realized how much she missed the natural daylight he enjoyed. Her ground-level studio had hardly any except on the sunniest days. She'd resorted to overhead lights intensifying her palette as compensation. It was not a totally unpleasant effect, advantageous rather, in that they'd evolved into deeper, richer statements. When she did have better light, her solution for achieving depth and luminosity would be nearer to resolution.

In the middle of the studio, glancing around again, breathing in its essence, Hattie was struck suddenly with a sense of calm as if she'd been cleansed. Like the feeling after bathing in a river, she felt purified and peaceful. With an overwhelming sensation of belonging, she had a sense of coming home after a tremendous journey. Raising her eyes she found Rex lolling against the wall across the room watching her as if he'd intercepted her chain of thoughts and sensed the significance of her revelation. It was one of the few times and places she'd been able to shed the protective wrapping that kept her distant, insulating her interior world from intrusion. Her emotions were exposed to the stranger, whom she instinctively trusted without reservation. She felt utterly naked and, minus the heavy armor, could experience fully the euphoria of freedom.

They stayed in the studio for a long time, talking about paintings and artists from the Renaissance to the present, finding to Hattie's surprise, a number of subjects on which they agreed.

He wanted to do some more painting before sunset, so she told him she'd go in search of the riding stables and possibly do some riding before dark. They would meet again later at the cottage for dinner.

Not far from the house she spotted a sign reading Horses for Rent, with an arrow below pointing inland, beside a path winding up through the dune grass. Following the trail she came to a clearing, almost like a large campsite, in the center of which was parked a long, narrow truck. Alongside it several horses were tied to a hitching post, saddled and bridled.

A scruffy-looking man in western riding gear was shoeing a horse in the back of the truck. As Hattie approached, he put down his tools, hopped down from the van and came over to her.

"Can I help you miss?" he asked in a lazy drawl.

"I'd like to take out one of your horses for a ride on the beach for about an hour," she replied. "I want the most spirited one you have."

"Well, none of them amounts to much in that department, I'm afraid, but of all of them, Caeser there is the liveliest," he said, pointing to a dark brown bay with a long black mane and tail.

Hattie walked over to the big, nearly black stallion and rubbed his soft, velvety nose. Snorting, gently tossing its head and pawing the ground, he greeted her skeptically. Not put off by its skittishness, Hattie flung her arms around his great neck and nuzzled into its musky mesh as if he were an old friend. The horse showed no signs of protest other than emitting a low, startled whinny and a guarded bonding was established.

Hattie paid the rental fee and led the horse beyond the field where the other horses were tied.

On the trail, she mounted, guiding him along the narrow grass path toward the beach. When they reached it, she edged close to the surf onto the hard, wet sand. They headed down the beach, running parallel with the sea.

From the start, Caesar wanted more reins than she was willing to give. Clearly he was used to having his head and she had to draw on all her strength to restrain him.

Finally somewhat quieted, he was a bit easier to control and they walked for a long time at a slow, steady gait. The sound of the horse's steps was completely obliterated by the drone of the breaking waves. It was just before sunset, Hattie's favorite time of day, a chance to draw the sea's essence into her intricate chambers, absorb its fragrance, its elemental forces, letting them flood her with the abandon of the tide coming into shore. The stillness, the gradually gentling waves, the harmony of rose-colored clouds against sky against sea against sand against shimmering pools of violet sea water, blanketed her like falling snow. The setting fiery-orange coal sank like a disc in quicksand, onto its nightly purple velvet cushion. But just before it reached home, it lit up the far side of the sea with a glittering, luminous glow.

Then, all at once, the sea, beach and sky were reeling past her like a rolling set, as the stallion broke free of his stranglehold. With the wind yanking at her hair, stinging her face, the two were charging wildly down the blurry beach, heedless of all but soaring rhythmically, in sync with the rush of pounding hooves and roaring surf.

On and on they flew, along the shore like a winged chariot keeping time with the flight of the seagulls. Racing in the gold-pink shadow stippled sand, they melted and ran together like magma flowing under the earth.

Mile after mile swept past them as they hurtled down the sandy runway, oblivious to all but a sense of buoyancy as they rushed headlong into the unexplored new territory.

Finally, winded, panting and snorting, the horse slowed its speed, giving Hattie a chance to catch her breath. Glancing around, she noticed a trail off to the left and turned the horse in its direction.

Following the path, they wound slowly up the mountainside. The higher they climbed, the rockier the surrounds became, making the going rough. Small patches of meadow flowers amid wild grass dotted the craggy slopes. Looking down over her shoulder, Hattie watched the sun's last rays sink below the horizon line far in the distance.

Coming to a plateau on the bluff, Hattie dismounted, allowing the horse to rest and graze as she stretched out in the meadow grass. From that vantage point her view of the ocean was unobstructed. She watched as twilight deluged the sea, casting an indigo calm across its breast, gently lulling it to sleep. Lying in dusk's hushed stillness her consciousness drifted like a glass float out to sea, until it reached the horizon, rolled over like a log at the crest of a waterfall and fell into an ethereal void.

It was very late when she woke. Quickly mounting, she and Caesar headed back down to the beach. Once there, they turned and rode briskly toward the riding camp, not slowing up until they reached it.

Spurred by hunger, the horse made rapid headway under Hattie's free rein. Just as darkness fell, they found the trail and forged up the clearing. Having deposited the horse, Hattie walked the short way back to the house.

From the beach she could barely discern its silhouette against the night sky by the glow streaming through the windows. Smoke spewed from the chimney in a long, unfurling spiral. Going around to the kitchen door, Hattie found Rex coming in with a load of wood. Opening the door, she followed him as he headed for the fireplace.

"I've reactivated this rusty old contraption in your honor," he said in his low, gruff voice, setting the logs down on the hearth and piling them on top of a kindling teepee stacked on the iron grate.

The dry wood burst instantly into flames throwing a gust of warmth over their chilled limbs. Hattie, never more content than when sitting in front of a fire, flopped down, Indian-style, on the floor as close as she could without crawling in.

Rex joined her, where they stared silently into the fire, letting it warm them like a potion, the flames dancing magically before them.

It was the most content Hattie had been for a long time. Seeing the radiant glow of happiness reflected on the shining contours of her face, Rex fell into a similarly languid, mellow mood. Intoxicated by her ebullient presence, he opened the floodgates of his spirit's inner sanctum pouring forth his boyhood experiences and dreams:

He was born in the small, country town of Sussex, New Hampshire. They established that, when Hattie was born, he was already a strapping six years old. His father had died of consumption when he was still very young and he, his mother, two brothers and three sisters had struggled along in financial straits for many years, barely able to survive. His mother, not well-educated, had gone to work in a cannery working long hours, often late into the night due to the erratic arrival times of the produce shipments. It was grueling, tedious, manual labor and she was often fatigued and irritable when she came in. Very little excitement or beauty brightened their existence, inducing Rex to fabricate a fantasy world of his own. Being the eldest of six children, he was called on often by his mother to help with chores and supervise the household while she was working or asleep. Still too young for a salaried job, he mowed lawns, weeded, gardened, chopped wood in the neighborhood to help with expenses.

Rarely, when he had an extra hour or two, he'd sneak off to the woods bordering the back section of town. Although he had a bicycle, he walked the long miles, using the time to conjure exotic gardens teeming with satyrs, nymphs, peacocks, doves and fountains, exquisite poetic places set in bucolic seclusion.

He surrendered to the wood's secret mysteries, its pines, birches, hemlocks, moss-covered logs, lily-encrusted ponds, ferns, lichens, wild flowers and each enchanted scent and sound. Ensconced in a clover patch, he dreamt of his life to be, of the day he'd venture into the world to carve out his place, of all the lovely things he would see and do.

All through high school, he worked every available hour saving up toward college. He didn't have much time to study, but his real education was the time spent exploring the wilderness, cultivating his imagination and gathering visual information useful for his future work. He chose a liberal arts college in New York where he studied art, art history and poetry. There, too, he worked to pay his expenses. Clerking every day after classes in the student bookstore, he was just barely able to eke out the needed funds to carry him through. Very little extra time remained for a social life or entertainment of any kind. He was locked into a fixed routine of working and studying. But every spare moment he went to the art building, set up easel, pulled out paints and canvas and painted. The rambling, Romanesque building provided the retreat where he served his apprenticeship. He walked its venerable halls with fresh purpose, belonging and confidence he was learning to exploit.

Every time he entered the art room he relished the soft light infiltrating arced windows lining the walls. But, mostly, he valued the exquisite peace saturating the atmosphere, rendering it quiet as a cloister.

His painting skills accelerated in the rarefied milieu that excluded all reminders of the outside world.

In that exalted space, he indulged his innermost fantasies, giving free play and scope to the imaginary visions of his dream world, a sometimes shocking range of emerging images. He worked prodigiously, and rather than tiring, his creative spirit rejuvenated each time he wielded a brush.

No one other than the art instructors and students ever saw his work. But their positive response, however guarded, buoyed him as if he'd been tossed a life raft.

By the end of his fourth year he'd saved enough for a year of postgraduate work.

During that period he met the instructor who would most influence him and his slowly burgeoning body of work.

Seth Sestina, Northwest painter and native Washingtonian, was Randolph University's resident artist, serving a year's nationally funded grant he'd recently accepted. His intricately woven tapestries of visionary mysticism were well-known and appreciated by Rex. Intrigued by one another's work, admiration and friendship developed between them and Rex drew heavily on his experience and art-world associations. They spent long hours talking, trading ideas, philosophies and secrets, even painting together. It evolved into an almost father-son relationship that proved a great source of inspiration and solace for Rex who'd lost his father so young. The older master recognized early the promise in the passionately expansive, romantic paintings of the younger man. He encouraged him to push and stretch his broadening vision and skills to the utmost. Rex's work flourished under his tutelage, bursting forth like an unopened blossom to the support and praise from his new friend and mentor. During the year, he expanded his repertoire of colors and imagery, not balking at any new influx of stimuli or unexplored creative avenue.

He tried every possible combination of colors and techniques until he uncovered his own visual symbols, strokes and marks. He proceeded undaunted, in an uninhibited display of artistic virtuosity.

At the end of the year he put several of his paintings in their first exhibition, a group show of student work held in a large, open room at the school. Wandering incognito among the viewers, he caught bits of remarks made by those standing in front of one of his creations. It was a mixed review.

Many were distracted by his innovative color. Unconventionally blended and applied, they didn't seem quite "right". Some were openly offended by their "offness" expecting them to be more "realistic". And some, threatened by the extravagantly aggressive brushstrokes, felt the images were jumping out at them. But a discriminating few were heartened by the freshness and vigor of his bold, new approach. Never had they experienced anything remotely like the clearly inspired visionary landscapes in their round of exhibits. In him they found a painter of definitive potential to watch.

Quiet as a mouse, he snuck out of the viewing room and went to a nearby bar to celebrate with a few beers. The remarks didn't affect him one way or another. His inner equilibrium remained stoically untouched by outside opinion, positive or negative. He'd formulated his own system, assessing and editing with savage ruthlessness. He spared himself no pain developing each painting, a process that often became as excruciating as blood-letting. If he heard disparaging remarks about his work they paled, compared to his own scathing critiques.

Walking back to his boarding house, the seeds for the blueprint of his future were germinating in his mind. Well aware that it might be many years before he could support himself with his art, if ever, he decided in the interim to teach, preferably college art. It was not a satisfactory alternative to painting. Painting would always come first in his heart and sacrificing any hours away from it would be painful. But the practical side of his poetic nature knew the need for prudence on the onset of his artful odyssey.

That unappetizing conclusion came concurrently with his arrival at the rooming house where he rented a tiny garret studio. He leadenly climbed its steep front steps, in the throes of a heavy malaise settling over him.

The tall brownstone, commonly called "The Muse" by its occupants, sat on a wide, tree-lined street overlooking the muddy green waters of the Horatio River.

He slowly climbed the three flights to his tiny flat, dropped his canvas and paint and stretched out on the draped sofa-bed. Feeling the fatigue of a thousand sleepless nights, he succumbed to the deep elixir of sleep, as to drams of some exotic potion.

Hours later, he slowly regained consciousness like some wild beast emerging from hibernation.

Consulting his watch he noticed it was dinnertime, when everyone congregated in the main dining hall. Even though he hadn't much appetite, he decided to go down anyway, hoping some company might lift his spirits.

The proprietress greeted him in the hallway as he descended the stairs. Plump, matronly and robust, she was known as Madame Ramelli. Of Italian descent, always merry and bright, she did all the cooking for the establishment. Mediterranean-style cuisine was her specialty which she was in the kitchen preparing, bustling cheerily over a huge pot of paella.

Usually it was Rex's favorite break in the day partly due to Madame Ramelli's hearty meals, partly to the large, airy dining room and partly to the coterie of artists, writers or poets.

Not very sociable in his present state, he chose a small table near a window looking out over the river. Several other men, already seated, briefly interrupted their heated discussion as he joined them. He dined in glum silence, the food tasteless and uninviting. He was in no mood to eat or talk, so he ate rapidly, noting indifferently that his moroseness was drawing attention. Used to his black moods, the others left him to his dark thoughts, and took up the thread of their debate. After a seemingly interminable time and having forced down as much as he could, he left as silently and gloomily as he'd come, little heartened by the respite. Climbing to his room once again, he lay down and immediately drifted into a fitful sleep.

The next afternoon, still in the grip of his depression and thinking it might buoy his flagging spirits, he went in search of a woman he was acquainted with in the art school. A first-year student, he recalled she worked part-time in the University's gallery museum and went there to find her.

The stately old Folsom Museum at the far edge of the campus stood in somber dignity on a main street leading to the business district. Tall and boxy, the Georgian-style stone mansion regally announced its main entrance with carved, ornamental windows, black wrought-iron gates and bronze-handled doors.

Just inside to the right was a small room housing art books, ethnic crafts, catalogues and framed posters of former exhibits. The woman was stationed behind the counter showing one of the museum's patrons a recent catalogue.

Rebecca Balcom had come to Randolph University as an art major from the town of Haddon, New Hampshire where she was born and had lived all her life. Everything about her fit into the medium range. She was medium-height, medium-weight, with medium-brown hair and eyes and of medium artistic ability. Because she was attractive, in a medium way, relatively well-read and one of the few women in the art department, Rex had slowly gravitated to her in frequent encounters at various common haunts. Not overly stimulated by her intellectually or physically, he was however, desirous of a friend on common ground who might lend a sympathetic ear.

When she spotted him, standing in the doorway, she appeared neither surprised nor particularly pleased to see him. Her features remained placid, almost sullen. He hoped, once they got acquainted, that she might rally, but wasn't certain that would happen. She glanced somberly toward him in acknowledgement. After her customer left he approached the counter.

"I was in the area and thought I'd drop by to see how you were doing," he ventured somewhat timorously. "I thought you might be ready to take a break and come have coffee with me."

Looking less intrigued than fatigued, she responded in her slow, halting, drawl-like manner, "I just have to balance the cash sheet and then I'll be through for the day. I could use a cup of coffee. I'll be right with you." And again she became immersed in her work.

Soon they were headed toward Dietrich's, a small coffeehouse near campus where the aroma of espresso never failed to revive Rex's spirit. He ordered café au lait, Rebecca a cappuccino, and then found a table in the back.

Once settled, they gratefully swallowed their first sips as Rex began telling her, in response to her query, about his latest works in progress.

They were, he told her, in a transitional stage. He was at work on new paintings very unlike previous ones in that they were based on real places he'd studied intimately in the region. Those done earlier were based more on memories of private, secret places from his boyhood in Sussex.

He was working larger, freer, looser, as a direct result of his apprenticeship with Northwest Master, Seth Sestina. But equally instrumental in his sudden breakthrough was deep inner searching, plumbing the depths with his inner eye, letting the mysteries emerge.

Rebecca listened intently to the story he ardently related, becoming more animated than he'd ever seen her. Being relatively well-acquainted with the Folsom Gallery's director besides Rex's former work, she silently considered suggesting he put one or more of his pieces in a group show. Rex watched her slip suddenly into the serious, pensive mood, guessing the vein of her thoughts and felt inwardly heartened.

She asked to visit his studio to see the latest paintings and, though he never let anyone into his sanctuary, found himself consenting to her plea as he gave directions to it on Cornwall Street. They set a time for the following week after classes and then, having finished their coffee, left the café and went their separate ways, she to the house she shared with several women and he, back to the boarding house.

After reaching his room, he followed the same pattern he had the night before only didn't bother going down to dinner. His appetite had flagged and he felt devoid of the energy to summon it even if he could. He merely strode slowly around the tiny space crowded with paintings, studying each as if seeing it for the first time with as impartial an eye as he could muster. Could they be ready for the Folsom Fine Arts Masters' show by spring?

He didn't know, but if not it would be no concern of his—disappointing, not catastrophic—and he might finish several large ones in time. The debilitating malaise was still upon him and, unable to concentrate on art anymore, he went to bed.

For the rest of the school year he fell into a strict regimen of painting, eating and sleeping. He painted strenuously, intensely, several hours every day usually in the art building, seeing few others except for the regular art students, Rebecca occasionally and the boarders.

He spent little time contemplating his current status or future outcome with Rebecca. He felt sure she wasn't seeing anyone else but, barely having time or energy for her, he feared the spark piqued in her would die of neglect. He'd have to take that risk because he had no intention of letting anyone or anything come between him and his art. It was always first in his mind and heart and he wouldn't sacrifice the slightest time he could be painting or drawing. He despaired of any lasting relationship with Rebecca. She was not overly anxious to be deterred from her own work which, he surmised, was one reason she wasn't more encouraging. They met for coffee, studio visits or an art exhibit, but only rarely, each extremely involved in his own art. She had less tuition money than he, spending more off-hours at jobs she was less than enthusiastic about, but helped pay her way.

Rex spent every spare moment in his studio conceptualizing, experimenting and executing his ideas.

One day Rebecca and Mr. LaMarr came to the studio to see his work. The director moved deliberately from painting to painting in silence, keenly absorbed in the work. Rex, not wanting to break his concentration, stood in the shadows, raptly observing the slightly unctuous LaMarr peruse the paintings, deeming them completely inscrutable.

It was soon clear to Rex that it was not a propitious time for the director to view his work. He had a final chance to scan his face as LaMarr turned back to him. The puzzled stare hovering there registered the same obtuseness he'd found embodied in Rex's paintings.

Obviously the paintings hadn't induced a favorable impression. Evidently it was the director's policy to say nothing if his reaction was negative, the catalyst, Rex assumed, for the glacial silence. He didn't return immediately to his painting after LaMarr and Rebecca left. His spirits were temporarily grounded and though he knew he could revive them enough to work, his concentration was too broken to work anymore that afternoon. That was the last time he would let anyone into his studio, he promised himself. Misunderstood and misinterpreted by the ignorant foreign element, he vowed his paintings to solitary confinement for the rest of the year. Following the infamous LaMarr studio visit he received a terse note from the director on the museum's distinctly monogrammed letterhead. It read in part that he appreciated seeing his work in progress, finding it "intriguing" and showing "indications" of great "promise". However, "at its present stage of development", somewhat lacking in "vitality and spontaneity of the palette" (misspelled pallete—his name, too, was misspelled Red), it would be premature to consider his work for inclusion in the annual group show. Perhaps closer to exhibition time if it were a "little further along in progress" he would be willing to reevaluate it. Rex had reread the letter several times in utter disbelief. His instincts sensed that the work had warranted more than the picayunish denouncement victimizing it. He spewed, seethed and raged, boiling inwardly at such drivel, at the petty diatribe by an effete bourgeois. Wadding up the piece of paper into a tight little ball, he heaved it out the window watching it, picked up by a gust of wind, sail across the street, disappearing over the bank.

After that demoralizing experience he turned more inward, devoting himself totally to the paintings. Delving deeper and deeper into himself, he tapped and transformed his inner vision into the distinctive "Dravus landscapes", as they were often dubbed. Sometimes working for more than twelve straight hours, he was intensely absorbed in reaching the images of his inner eye and imprinting them on canvas before they could slip away and lose the impact of their initial force. He worked in a trance-like fever, with the rhythm of incoming waves coursing through him.

The only permanent fixture in his existence was the fallow well of sadness in the depths of his core, to be dredged up by some flickering figment of the past. Rather than hampering his ability to function, its infernal presence had become second nature, like newly molted snakeskin. He'd learned not only to live with it, but to ignore it, obscuring its potential mischief to the point of obliteration. When it threatened him, he grappled with the malevolent demon in an internal tug-of-war battling for survival. But more often it lay wallowing like sediment in a stagnant swamp, harmless until stirred.

He painted volcanically, summoning every sinew until he was drawing upon pure blood and marrow for his inspiration. The paintings reflected the intense dedication that was rapidly becoming his hallmark. The composite insignia of every piece was its stamp of quality and consummate skill. Privately he compared it with another phenomenon of similar profundity—the birthing process. He felt certain he'd undergone the same degree of anxiety, excruciating pain and expended effort as a woman endured in the throes of delivery.

He wrestled with the new work through the remaining year, branding each fresh image onto the canvas before it could vanish. Feverishly he brandished his brush until he'd transmitted his last vestiges of passion.

The recent work completed, he suffered the usual post-partum gloom and, as follow-up therapy, tried to drown his doldrums in alcohol.

Six months had passed since Rebecca and the infamous LaMarr blitzed his studio.

One day Rebecca stopped by alone to see the works-in-progress. Unlike her last visit, though more sympathetic than the museum director, she was completely overwhelmed. Both her awe and excitement were palpable in the cramped, poorly lit studio. A surge of adrenaline from the paintings' powerful impact washed over her. She was speechless, able only to stand in reverence before the virtuoso display of truth, light and beauty.

Each creation radiated its own incandescence, unique, yet harmoniously intermingling with the others, inducing in Rebecca the strong impression that the entire body was nothing less than a Promethean labor of love.

It took all her persuasive powers to convince Rex that it was his duty to the art community and the art world in general to exhibit them, adding that Mr. LaMarr also should see them immediately.

Mumbling to himself, he finally agreed, reasoning that he had more to gain than lose from the unveiling. They scheduled the director's next visit, then went out for a welcome, if premature, celebration.

Henry LaMarr, studying the paintings on his second visit, instantly noticed tremendous progress. He grudgingly admitted to himself that there was merit in them. In fact he finally concurred with Rebecca that they really were quite good.

His nagging complaint concerned Dravus's concentration on spontaneity at the expense of technical detailing. But more pronounced than before was the broad scope of mood and gesture that collectively expunged his more basic concerns. He spent nearly two hours carefully perusing every piece, taking note of the pros and cons of each. After according them, theoretically, his most objective analysis, in practice purely subjective, he posed exhibiting in the Masters' spring show to Dravus. Rex accepted, suppressing his prior hostility toward the fatuous director, helping select five paintings to be included. LaMarr, of more conservative taste, leaned toward the least bold or ambitious pieces. But Rex vigorously, often eloquently, defended his choices, eventually swaying the director to his side and the subject was, somewhat ungraciously, closed.

Rex dressed the works in simple wood frames and delivered them to the gallery with just time for the show to be hung and opened.

Rebecca, by then more than professionally interested in Rex, supplied him with viewers' reactions by strategically stationing herself about the gallery.

The prognosis was still split as before, but good comments clearly outdistanced bad. In fact, she happily related, his paintings were causing quite a ripple. Art students as well as professionals were seeing the show, specifically his work and weren't disappointed, judging from their absorption. She reported some spent their entire time studying his paintings, while others stood gazing rapturously in a trancelike state.

Rebecca was greatly excited and heartened by the positive reception, but Rex, ever the skeptic regarding public opinion, remained unmoved. Still, she thought she detected slight signs that secretly he was pleased, his spirits buoyed by the commotion.

With the show's relative success and LaMarr's offer to show regularly at the Folsom, Rebecca and Rex felt more confident to step up the pace of their deepening intimacy.

"Will you come live with me and be my love?" he asked playfully one day soon after, and she readily said she would.

They quickly gathered up their things—for him, mostly paintings and her few belongings—at their respective lodgings and moved to a tiny house not far away on Edgewater Road. It wasn't much more than a shack of dark, cedar shingles weathered to a dull gunmetal gray. The shake roof sagged in places and there was only one main room plus a tiny bedroom. But, at the end of a cul-de-sac, it was quiet, surrounded by several huge, old hemlocks. They could glimpse the river from a small-paned window in the kitchenette that held no more than one wood counter, cupboards and an old wood stove, the only source of heat.

They settled in quickly, owning so little and contentedly continued the arrangement of study, work and, Rex, his painting. Each night at dusk, after classes and part-time jobs, they met and walked back to the house along the river. The sinking sun dropped a spangled golden net over fuschia water.

It was their hour to unwind from the day's pressures, share their problems and joys, but mostly it was for formulating and unveiling their plans and dreams.

Rex had just finished his fifth year. He told Rebecca of his many long talks with Seth Sestina and with what fervor he spoke about the quality of life in the Northwest. Sestina had fished its lakes, rivers and streams, trekked into the Rainbow and Sylvania mountains, sailed on Webster Bay and Norfolk Sound, explored the Osprey Peninsula, the rainforest, all the national parks and the several Indian reservations where thousands of artifacts and relics had been unearthed.

And Rex, avid outdoorsman, fisherman and climber with an inordinately fertile imagination, was enthralled by Sestina's tales, felt compelled to see the great frontier for himself.

Rex's passionate descriptions detailing life out west acted like an opiate on Rebecca, soon embroiled in the same web of intrigue surrounding its grandeur and mystery.

During those riverside strolls the two lovers charted the course of their expedition to Washington. They decided to work until they could afford to transplant their lives. By the end of summer they hoped to have enough to buy a jalopy to haul them to the hinterland.

Once they'd decided to move, the means to that end loomed menacingly, then settled into grim drudgery. Bleakly they plodded through the days, disgruntled with their jobs and environs, anxious to embark on their odyssey.

Classes over, they stretched their work to full-time. By August, spotting an antiquated hauling van, they pooled their wages to buy it with some left over for fuel.

By September, they'd paid off their back rent, loaded the van, shipped Rex's paintings to one of Sestina's colleagues and begun the first leg of their journey. Heading first to Washington, D.C., they spent several long days, wandering the National Gallery's serpentine chambers studying the Old Masters and Impressionists, the latter of particular interest to Rex. Rebecca, drawn more to the garden courtyard, fountains and sculpture, left Rex to his solitary inquiry into the magic of Monet, Renoir and Cezanne.

After digesting the delicacies offered by the august museum, they left for Boston's Isabella Stewart Gardner Museum. Rex rhapsodized over the splendor of Raphael, Titian and Rembrandt, and again Rebecca devoted more time to the architecture, courtyards and fountains than to the paintings.

When Rex suggested they see the national cemetery at Gettysburg, Rebecca longed to refuse but grudgingly agreed. What had the Civil War Memorial to do with her, she petulantly asked herself. But Rex urged until her childish defenses collapsed and they set off. He found his paternal great-grandfather's name enrolled among the voluminous list of fallen warriors and felt soothed knowing he'd been so nobly laid to rest. Rebecca barely glanced at any of it, still sulking about the unwelcome detour. From Pennsylvania they headed southwest to the gulf coast, driving down through the northwest tip of Alabama, cutting a diagonal slash across it and Mississippi, over the Texas Panhandle, into New Mexico. Once in New Mexico they visited the grave of D. H. Lawrence, whose writings they both admired, and spent hours roaming through galleries in Santa Fe and Taos. Rebecca, indifferent to most of the art and craftsmanship of both native and transplant, preferred the architecture and vegetation, leaving Rex to his usual solitary pursuits. By that time he'd become increasingly annoyed at Rebecca's incessant nagging. It was either too hot, too cold, too wet or too dry. She was hungry, thirsty, too tired to travel or the van's sleeping quarters were too cramped. Rebecca, meanwhile, with ample time to study Rex closely, noticed his thorough preoccupation with art and painting and lack of concern for her.

At last they were driving along the final stretch, barely speaking. Their spirits were greatly lifted as they traveled north along the Coast Highway with its dizzying heights, view of the Pacific and winding curves among cliffs, canyons and forests. They sped along to the strains of Bach, Beethoven, Chopin and Brahms through most of California and all of Oregon. Suddenly they met the Columbine River and crossed it into Washington. They snaked past woods and mountains to Sealth, home of the state's largest city, university and Seth Sestina.

In town Rex steered down to the waterfront's old section where Sestina's friend had a studio-loft.

Even though it was late, they saw lights in the artist's studio. Rex had telephoned from the border telling him they'd be in that night.

Casey Banyan's studio sat at the head of steep, narrow stairs next to an all-night diner. The entrance was reached by a secret, brooding midnight-blue door. Slightly recessed, its façade was deeply scarred, ostensibly at the hands of passing street people or unrulies of the metro shelter sitting before it. As if disturbed by the intrusion, it had to be given a hefty shove before granting admission. Just inside was a tiny causeway, reeking of filth, then another, heavier door mottled with whitewash and graffiti. Pulling that open, light and warmth poured forth and a soft nocturne floated down as Casey Banyan grinned welcomingly from above.

Tall, thin and slightly distinguished looking, there was an elfish elegance about him.

Behind him sprawled the studio loft, radiant and purring in the diffused warmth of overhead lights. The far end of the long, narrow room lay sheathed in darkness. Ficus silhouettes lurked in the shadows, looming like centaurs from mammoth clay vessels.

A greeting committee of huge, splashy canvases leaned against the walls, a riotous consortium of unsullied reds, blues and yellows. Charcoal sketches covered large stark blocks of paper tacked to the walls. The living quarters alcove beside the staircase held bookcases, a bed, oak table and a sparsely filled portable clothes rack. Just across the passway, the tiny kitchen, divided from the studio by a makeshift partition, faced a wood counter lined with bar stools; small appliances, a two-tiered shelf stuffed with spice bottles and food staples hovered against a backdrop of tall windows that ran in a continuous row around the studio. Some were draped in canvas, others shrouded in bamboo blinds to filter out harsh daylight. Little touches like the wine bottle on the countertop, literally the first thing one saw, contributed to the pleasure of being in Casey Banyan's studio.

They sipped wine at the counter, relying heavily on mutual-friend Sestina to bridge the awkward gap. A long wine, music and conversation interlude later, Rex and Rebecca brought in some things for their short stay with Casey Banyan. They set up camp under the potted trees, spreading out blankets, sleeping bags and pillows on the drafty wood floor. During the following days they would search for a home of their own.

Early the next day, at Casey's suggestion, the three drove north for about two hours through some of the best backcountry Rex had ever seen. Casey explained they were in the Indio Valley, one of the state's most special sections, known for its flowers, horses and wildlife. Rex and Rebecca were instantly seduced by its unspoiled natural beauty. Everywhere were wide open spaces—fertile livestock-grazed pastures, rivers, mountains, tall grass fields, wildflowers and Norfolk sound, glimpsed in the distance.

They drove in the country all day, through surrounding resort towns on the water with their relaxed insouciance attracting hordes of tourists. Fittingly most of the adjoining farms cultivated flowers instead of vegetables, grain, poultry or beef, harvesting huge plantation-scale crops of tulips and daffodils.

Then, after scouring the area for hours, they spotted a little spread delineated by a split-rail fence. A small, neglected log cabin sat nestled amidst an ancient oak grove. There weren't any signs of life, as if abandoned for a long time. Rampant-growing grass, tall as the bottom rung of the front porch, choked out everything around its foundation. Peering in through the front window they saw the stone fireplace and scarred floor but little else. Behind the house a small shed and sparse orchard of gnarly, old fruit trees sat beside a meandering brook, its banks tangled with overgrown vegetation.

They found a sign posted on the shed door with a broker's number which they immediately jotted down, grateful for a clue about the property.

Tired but obsessed by his latest pursuit, Rex consulted Rebecca briefly, determined to possess the place, or at least be well along by day's end.

They drove almost ten miles to the town listed on the broker's card and finally found the realty office. Not long after they were meeting the agent, a trifle ruffled that his prospective clients had arrived so near quitting time. But never jeopardizing a potential sale, he answered the restless stranger's queries about the old Bradford place. They spent the next hour going over the deed, mortgage, financing, taxes and insurance. Deliberating only briefly, Rex signed the earnest agreement along with the down payment check. The agent agreed to their moving in within two weeks since they'd just arrived from out of state and were camping out in a temporary housing. Excited by their new land baron status, they cajoled Casey into taking them out on the town. So, climbing into Rex's beat-up van, the three set out in search of some libation.

Soon a smattering of lights shone ahead as they neared El Paseo, Indio Valley's tiny centerpiece. At its hub, two-and-a-half blocks of small but thriving concerns, they were magnetically drawn to the El Paseo Saloon, its busiest watering hole. Although Casey knew the El Paseo's reputation as a haunt for painters, writers, poets and other local celebrities, he regretted never having been in it. It provided a refuge for artists in which to vanquish their various demons through liquor, the attentions of local admirers, a colleague's empathetic ear or, more often, all three. Familiar with much of El Paseo artists' work from exhibits in Sealth and studio visits, Casey didn't take long to identify the familiar faces of several veterans in the dim light. He instantly gravitated to the deeply etched face of the legendary painter, Ben Toucan. The scene before them was picaresque if somewhat primitive. Huge old landscapes, esoteric symbols of Indian folklore and other local relics dominated the rustic log walls. Painted totem poles, semi-obscured in the dimness, stood, majestic and proud, like noble mascots, at regular intervals around the room. Handed down through generations of Indian craftsmen living and working on coastal reservations, they'd gradually found their way to the famous establishment.

The three newcomers sat at the massive bar's hand-hewn counter beside the elusive Toucan. They fell quickly into step with his voice's melodious rhythm as he recounted early exploits around the valley. Like a repertory actor captivating his audience, he held them with the powerful tool of a rich, resonant cadence added to the stories' colorful drama. They listened, spellbound, as he skipped from tale to tale, finding them a little more attentive than they were as he moved deftly on to the next.

Aladdinlike, perched atop his barstool like a great bald eagle guarding his brew, Ben Toucan ushered forth fable after fable from his fathomless storehouse of material. Issued up, one genie after another, they enchanted the rapt listeners who were alternately shocked and intrigued. Finally, drained, the trio headed back to Sealth and Casey's studio, singing bawdy barroom ballads most of the way. Once again in the studio they had little energy to do anything except crawl into bed, sleeping far into the next morning. Casey's usual midday ritual of rustling up a huge country-style breakfast promptly stirred Rex and Rebecca with its aroma.

Sitting together at Casey's counter, they were too busy stuffing themselves to talk much. Casey's faithful cassette sent out faint shades of Stravinsky's Firebird. After breakfast Casey took them on a walking tour of Old Town abutting his studio's building on all three sides.

Many streets still touted original cobblestones dating from the city's birth nearly a century before. Ornately carved lamp-posts crowned by huge round globes lined most streets, lending a magic ambiance. Each stone or brick building, snugly nestled along the tree-lined walks, had its own unique facade and history. The wide variety of ethnic restaurants created an international flavor. Treed and cobbled Central Plaza sprawled at Old Town's nave. The sculpted fountain drew indigent souls en masse to camp on its encircling cement benches. They were lulled into stupors by drink and the sound of rushing water. The lumpy-stoned square was the meeting ground for enterprising pigeons greedily snapping up leftovers. A lavishly appointed French brasserie's garden pavilion jutted out onto the courtyard. Every evening its crystal chandeliers, glowing jewels in a great glass case, illuminated tree clusters and cobbles of the bohemian Eden surrounding it.

Casey led them down crowded St. Charles Street, across from the plaza and entrance to the Royal Grand Hotel's shopping arcade. At St. Charles' southwest corner stood Webster Bay Books, one of Casey's special haunts that he wanted to show his new friends. It was packed, as usual, with milling browsers, tables and stalls stacked with books, magazines, pamphlets, maps and catalogues. Warm and brightly lit, it smelled of coffee and baking. A central staircase in the main room led down to the café and espresso bar sharing space with used books. Overstuffed shelves of musty tomes lined the walls around marble-top tables and battered chairs. The floor was inlaid with antique mosaic tiles. Spots of bright paintings gaily punctuated the walls. Casey gravitated there often, drinking coffee non-stop while leafing through books which occasionally, to his delight, turned out to be rare. The three plunked down at a table near the back, their plates covered with cheesecake, pie, whipped cream and cups of bitter espresso. An ingratiatingly lazy charm wove a spell of enchantment over everyone causing them to lean back and stretch out with contented sighs.

Rex surveyed the place, surprised by a buoyancy creeping over him. Meeting magic by chance always excited him. He glanced at Rebecca, noting her strange indifference. Ignoring her mood and the glum way she was poking pieces of pie around her plate, he stretched his legs and sipped the steaming brew.

He and Casey discussed the move to Indio Valley within two weeks, Casey offering his loft until the sale was complete, to Rex's relief. In the interim he would scout through the art community for a prospective gallery. Casey, acquainted with them all and most of the owners, wanted to see his work to better connect him with a suitable showcase and introduce him to dealers. The next day he and Casey set out. The first two were totally unacceptable. The first gallery, atop a narrow flight of steps in an historic brick building in the heart of Old Town, displayed three bodies of work of uneven quality in three rooms. The second gallery exploited proficient, if somewhat anemic, products by the art community's academic branch. The third turned out to be the charm. The moment Rex walked through the massive black front door, a sense of warmth and hospitality washed over him. The atmosphere, rather than opulent, exuded friendly unpretension. A small mutt danced a frenzied, sniffing greeting around their feet. The rooms weren't distinctive but high-ceilinged and bright. Something glowed about them. It wasn't the innocuous gold carpet, nor anything elegant. But a luminous element, an ethereal spirit that pervaded the space moved Rex, drawing him toward the exhibit. Soft music perfectly accompanied his viewing.

He concentrated on the work, finding it fully absorbing. Most of the canvases were large, exuberant fields of vibrant color, briefly delineated by flowing lines. Fluid, visionary, the paintings swept him along, seducing him with their poetic lyricism.

After according the show his critical expertise, Rex knew instinctively it was the space he'd been searching for from the start.

He and Casey talked with the co-owners for a long while as Rex showed samples of his work which they responded to immediately. They soon saw he would be a stellar attraction in their stable. Accomplished, gifted, producing powerful, compelling work, he also possessed considerable personal magnetism. Their enthusiasm over his pieces was infectious, taking Rex by surprise, catching him slightly off-guard. Usually the reception was more ambivalent. But recovering quickly, he offered to bring in several more paintings from the van to give them a wider range to inspect. They were obviously eager for the chance. He brought in three works from the "Woods" series in varying shades of green, tinged with touches of violet, blue-violet and purple. Bearing the Dravus mark of mystery and introspection, they were boldly arresting. Wilson and Pearson stood before them, momentarily stunned by their power, drawn within the rhythmic passages, into the deepest chambers of their soul. Nothing remotely equaling their virtuosity had crossed their paths in years. They clumsily tried to tell Rex of the great affinity his paintings had elicited, to his relief and secret delight.

Only the matter of the contract remained, required between the gallery and each of its artists. Rex, warned by both Sestina and Banyan against signing away his copyrights, was fully versed and ready to wage war for adequate remuneration and control. When Pearson and Wilson presented him with gallery terms to study and sign, he balked at any binding restrictions. The commission issue was straightforwardly presented and not Rex's major concern. The gallery would retain fifty percent of retail unless the artist assisted with press releases, mailing and hanging. In that event, it would be forty per cent, fairly standard conditions for most galleries. The agreement further stipulated an exclusive gallery option on the exhibiting artists to show and sell with it alone. Rex, though not an aggressive marketer, was well known by the art community and had ample opportunity to show and solicit his work. He finally compromised with the reluctant dealers. He would retain the right to exhibit and sell his work in other states or internationally. Finally, satisfied with the settlement, Rex and Casey gathered up the paintings and went out to celebrate.

They made their way from midtown back to Old Town to the Casablanca. Pushing their way through the double doors the first thing they always saw was a giant black and white image of Humphrey Bogart leering sardonically from beneath his black-banded Homberg, wearing the signature tan trench coat. Several other poses of him were scattered around the room. A huge video screen peered down from the back corner like a security scanner. Several steps led up to the pool table platform. Cedar walls, pink lights, jukebox, bottle-lined bar shelves, tables and chair clusters in front and side rooms, tortilla chips with salsa sauce and pounding rock music filled the space.

Rex and Casey had a ritual, the grand finale, of ordering a shot of whiskey followed by one last beer chaser. They were usually flocked by reverent art students meeting weekly at Casey's for life drawing from the nude, hoping to follow their mentor's path to fame and glory.

Not drawing session night, Casey and Rex had time to think, relax and drink in peace.

They'd discovered long ago there wasn't much common ground on which they agreed. Their backgrounds and philosophies were as diverse as their paintings. So they'd learned to say little, to commune on a plane of silent bonding as they were then in the process of doing. Casey Banyan was a spritelike elf compared to the brooding Dravus. Banyan was well-read and thoroughly versed on art but a semi-malicious sourness ran through him, creating a disturbing amiable animosity. In fact he'd deliberated so little on the mysteries and intricacies of life and the human psyche, that he had no real concept of himself. Over the years he was disintegrating into a walking shell, the mere shadow of the idealistic boy he'd once been. Rex, conversely, was so immersed in his own inner meanderings that he often lost sight of all else around him.

He spent increasing amounts of time, usually far into the night, engrossed in his work, nearly dropping from fatigue, sleeping in an exhausted heap in the midst of his paintings. Nothing took precedence over his art. He became a living, breathing production machine, churning out one creation after another until his imaginative juices temporarily flagged. So, as he and Casey sat at the table at the Casablanca staring emptily into one another's eyes each was caught up with his own demons and angst plaguing the inner world of creative spirits.

The Wilson/Pearson Gallery scheduled Rex for July, almost eight months to prepare. Already he could feel the creative juices flowing, the familiar stirring in his blood, racing heart and turbulent mind urging him on to start the new paintings. He was already picturing the clean expanse of canvas that never failed to thrill him, the imagery, the palette he would transform into the vision of his inner eye. It was becoming harder for him to sit still when he could be releasing raging forces gathering momentum.

Swigging down one last shot of searing whiskey, he indicated to Casey that he was ready to turn in. Casey, following suit, gulped from his shot glass and the two headed outside, crossing the street to Casey's loft. Rebecca was already asleep at the far end of the studio when Rex joined her. She grudgingly acknowledged him with an impatient groan and flopped onto her side.

Rex kept his distance, knowing her cantankerous mood when interrupted in sleep and soon, was wracked in his own fitful slumber.

By morning he felt revived and more determined than ever to leave immediately for the Indio Valley. Casey fixed them a farewell country-style breakfast, then helped them gather their belongings together and cart them to the van. By mid-morning they'd said goodbye and were on the interstate to their new home. Two hours later they finally spotted the tiny, overgrown spread on the outskirts of El Paseo. It looked like paradise to Rex who'd kept its essence alive since the first moment he'd spied it. He pulled into the grass drive, firmly flicked off the engine and stepped from the van filled with optimism, feeling every inch the lord of the manor.

They climbed up rickety steps, removed the padlock and opened the battered front door.

Rex fell instantly under its spell. His first chore was to light a fire in the small, debris-strewn fireplace. He ran outside gathering up bits of twigs and scraps like a modern Robinson Crusoe. Loading up, he carried them to the rusty, old grate, lovingly arranging them as if the first primate to rub sticks together.

Rebecca set about fixing dinner in the little, galleylike kitchen. Even though caught up in the commotion of settling in, they'd remembered to bring in food for a few days' meals. Not particularly fond of cooking or the least domesticated, Rebecca grimaced at the primitive conditions. The place was filthy with neglect and she wondered if her paralyzed appetite would ever return. Old paint peeled from every surface, countertops were sheathed in disgusting gold-specks, wallboard was cracked and falling and dirt-mottled linoleum obscured the floor. The cupboards were warped and ajar and she cringed to touch the appliances. The only bright spot, though coated with grime, was the small-paned window looking out on the orchard and kitchen garden. Flinging it open with a wave of relief, she willed in the late afternoon sun and fresh air as if exorcising traces of former occupants through some ancient tribal rite.

They dined simply on ground beef, succotash and salad, on an old crate in front of the fireplace. One candle lit the ritual, blocking out most of the dishevelment to lend a romantic air.

Rex's jubilant first night in his new home was tainted as he saw, in the dim glow, Rebecca's twisted features molded in disappointment fringed with disgust. That moment he realized she would never, could never, share his vision, understand the yearning embedded in his soul for the rustic life. Her face, the thoughts behind which he'd learned to read so well, registered every faded dream of the child, the young girl she'd once been. They were lofty notions of a fanciful dreamer lost in imaginary wanderings among magical kingdoms;

of sandcastles, palaces, villas in the midst of exquisite gardens, fountains and peacocks; of everything lovely in the unattainable netherland.

She was so far beyond his reach, as he sought some sign of intimacy, that he soon descended into one of his profoundest moments of despair. He was sure she was lost to him forever, that they would never commune quite the same again. And when he raised his eyes, hers told him unflinchingly that he'd deciphered her feelings perfectly.

For a short time there was relative harmony between them as they struggled to establish a habitable, if not comfortable, home. The tasks at hand seemed endless, sometimes grueling, but temporarily usurped their personal conflicts.

Rex soon fell into a rhythmic pattern of painting long, arduous hours everyday. Everything else, including Rebecca and the mounting demands of homemaking, came second. He refashioned the old shed behind the house clearing it completely of all but paintings and materials. He cut through the sagging, shingled roof, installing a huge slab of small, wood-framed glass panes. The north light filtering in illuminated his realm with diffused radiance, turning it into the rarefied loftiness of an ancient cathedral.

From then on he concentrated nearly every waking moment on his easel, devising, refining, innovating. Immersed in dreams he, like one of Michaelangelo's Slaves, struggled toward freedom, soared toward enlightenment, to his vision's ideal. The peace pervading the property acted like an opiate unleashing his pent-up creative forces, surging them suddenly into motion again like an unfurled log jam.

He worked as never before, completely absorbed, purposeful, single-minded, wracked with dredging up an essence intact, often foregoing mundanities like eating or sleeping. He ate, he slept, but grudgingly, sporadically and only when his body rebelled, demanding attention before it would continue. The work gushed fecundly, steeped in the freshness of a tropical rainforest after a torrential downpour.

He spent hours investigating the valley. Revived, his life's blood coursed through him, revitalized him, making him feel young and carefree. Memories of adventurous, uninhibited childhood forays into the New Hampshire woods flooded his mind. Hurtled back in time, he was once more that small-mystified creature awed by the magic around him. All traces of tension vanished. His limbs and spirit buoyant, he peeled away the layers of armor, feeling feather light, warm, good and twelve years old again.

In the days and months that followed, the strain of living with Rebecca weighed heavily on Rex. His only solace was the refuge of work, fueling Rebecca's discontent in knowing his art was her greatest rival. Its allure was the one mistress she could never compete with and the tighter its hold over Rex became, the more hers slackened.

Day by day his commitment to his work deepened as his to Rebecca waned. He felt shut out of her mind and heart by her increasing alienation. Little by little, she'd lost all hope of recapturing the intimacy they knew in the beginning. She watched helplessly as he drifted further and further away until he was beyond her reach.

He painted everyday but less often found his studio the tranquil sanctum it had once been. Rebecca would barge in with some trifling concern or complaint and upset the equilibrium he'd wrought so painstakingly within its confines.

More and more often he took his paints and brushes and headed out into the valley. Setting up his easel he tried to capture the lush abundance spread about him. So numerous were the subjects that he felt overwhelmed at first, fearing he might not do their sublimity justice.

He braved on, hauling out sheet after sheet of drawing paper. Sketching broadly, he quickly slashed the charcoal against the paper until its whiteness submitted to the bold lines valiantly overtaking it. As soon as he got one image down he rushed on to the next, frantic to seize the scent before the light changed. He worked frenziedly against the shifting elements, forced to adopt freer, simpler strokes, stretching to gain greater spontaneity and vitality.

Organic rocks, trees, fields of flowers rose out of the blank, white void charged with charisma. Barns, chapels, walls, bridges chiseled by his brush exuded solidity and integrity. But rendered most dazzling and unique were rivers, streams, clouds, skies, sunrises, sunsets. Ingenuity and elemental forces suffused his atmospheres with soulful sensitivity, moving them from mere sentiment to profundity.

Daily he labored to infuse the poetic vision being transfixed onto canvas with the same magic as the original. Daily he pursued truthful renderings of his subjects and daily he progressed further toward his ideal.

After several days he'd often traveled so far from home that he was forced to camp out in his van stranded in some field, lulled to sleep by the stars' rhythmic glittering. Those frequent stopovers allowed him the freedom and immediacy to experience the valley swathed, first in moonlight, then in dawn.

And with his increased nocturnal outings came the gradual deterioration of his relationship with Rebecca. She'd never fully forgiven him for not insisting on marriage and each subsequent misdemeanor compounded that original sin. When he explained that his sometimes-extended stays in the wilds were necessitated by the hour, she was more vexed than consoled.

The days turned into weeks, then months and still Rex refused to abandon, or even alter, his work pattern. It had risen in stature to his primary raison d'être. It alone could be trusted, was always there, stood by him not only during fruitful times but lean ones as well. It became his sole constant companion, striving with him toward a heightened state of being.

He spent only brief times with Rebecca, when he wasn't painting, commuting to Sealth or making the rounds in El Paseo. Their union, instead of seasoned by time, slowly eroded like a surf-worn crag consumed by the sea.

They watched helplessly as the foundation of their disintegrating love collapsed and fell.

They were strangers again. Self-consciousness in each other's company became the norm. They sensed the end by the solicitous way they treated one another, mincing words, tiptoeing around as if walking on eggshells. The atmosphere at home felt, to Rex, strained, tense and intolerable. He stretched his time away to last longer than the time there. He focused his energy and attention on the Wilson/Pearson exhibit scheduled to open in six months. He wouldn't allow domestic unrest to deter him from triumph on that front. He began the work in earnest, with the same intensity and care but newly impassioned. His feverish effort was that of a drowning man with a harbinger of his fate if he didn't succeed.

His exuberance in the open fields crept into his art, fresh and vigorous as his own state of mind. Losing all concept of time, ageless, tireless, he was propelled by the fertile depths of his imagination.

He'd never painted so freely, charting a new course filled with grace and purity. Subdued yet deep, the cast of his colors shone with a delicate, subtle elegance. He was continually discovering new ground on which to build, incorporating previously unexplored techniques and theories. And once those had been mastered he was already restlessly trying to surpass them. Rarely satisfied with his offspring, he refused to let an iota of stasis seep in. He'd add, retouch, wipe out, then reject the whole to start again, rarely leaving one long enough to dry and, rarer still, letting one stay as it was.

Using that modus operandi meant a more slowly accrued output. He worked steadily, almost obsessively, completing twenty various-size paintings within eight months. There was only time for framing before they were due at the gallery for hanging.

In his studio, putting his brushes aside temporarily, he soon shifted everything to his current purpose. Looking more like a carpentry shop, it was quickly crammed with woodworking tools. The room was alive with sawhorses, table saws, corner braces, clamps and thin wood strips. Rex, on the brink of exhaustion, rather relished a brief respite from the rigors of painting, slipping easily into his carpenterial guise.

Framing was child's play compared to the Herculean labor of painting. By contrast, woodcutting, gluing, clamping, nailing and stringing hanging wire were elementary.

Applying his shop skills he was finished in a week, leaving only another week until delivery.

He hung up his tools, donned his angling garb, grabbed his gear and set out for the hallowed grounds.

He drove almost ten miles to the Mohecan River, the Indio's great irrigator and richest fishing bed. Trampled banks testified to its sanctity among the seasoned swarms of sportsmen.

The current mirrored his spirit's wild pursuit of adventure and freedom.

No one else was at the river. Inflating his float and pulling on his hip boots, he waded in. The sun cast a shadowy maze, mottling illusory nooks and crannies, emboldening the fish with false security. Rex, like all veterans, hovered near dark spots tucked in between large rocks or tall, reedy marsh grass. Luckily he and the fish arrived together. In a little while he caught his limit, released most, kept a few. At that hour the marked calm numbed his raw nerves, luxuriantly lolling him in delicious repose. The angst seeped away as his sense of virility and vitality resurged.

At night he slept in his van, fished mornings, wiled away the days with isolated abandon, cherishing the tranquility. Flourishing, he wondered would he ever want to leave paradise for the urban jungle awaiting him?

But by the end of the fifth day, as if by rote, he resolutely packed up and headed back to his art, the one thing he could never totally desert.

Working rapidly, he raced against the deadline. With only a day to wrap and pack his paintings, he had no time to lose, breaking only to eat.

Early the next morning he was on his way to Sealth, the van loaded down with the fruits of his labor. By midday he'd delivered them to the gallery where they'd been anxiously awaiting him. Perturbed by his last minute arrival, they had only that afternoon to mount the show. With his help, the work went fast. Rex had envisioned the exact order the paintings should be arranged. Wilson and Pearson wasted no time arguing, giving minimal input as to lighting and spacing. The hanging of the entire show took a little over three hours. Twenty diverse canvases, mostly large, glowed against their stark backdrop. A smattering of charcoal drawings and smaller works rested below the larger pieces. The paintings' impact, viewed in their entirety was immediate and dramatic. With a sweeping glance, Wilson and Pearson were again struck by the artist's genius. The works' bold, dynamic force surpassed their wildest hopes, perfuming the air with the smell of success.

Morning broke, jolting Rex awake with a sickening churning in the pit of his belly. Jarring daylight catapulted him upright in his bed on Casey Banyan's floor. Disoriented, he stumbled toward the breakfast bar for coffee to start him on the road back to life. Sometime during his morning shower-shaving-robing ritual he began to resume a rather halting momentum. Somewhere during this third cup he snapped fully awake, moving more purposefully. Thoughts of the gallery, beckoning like a flare in the fog, flooded his body with the juices of resolve, propelling him forward. It was going to be a long day.

The big man, his jaw jutting determinedly, hurtled his van through the crowded city toward the gallery with the gusto of a mistral.

Once inside he heaved a huge sigh of relief. They were all there, just as he'd left them, pouring forth gentle strains in silent salutation.

The gallery hummed with activity. Workmen looking more like high wire acrobats in striped overalls, formed strange contortions adjusting overhead lights from their ladders. Window washers stripped the grimy glaze off the front windows, even polished the massive, lion-head knocker. Nothing was left unchecked under Skip Wilson's deft direction. Burt Pearson heralded florists hugging potted palms and bowls of flowers to designated sites tucked about the rooms. Technicians tested and tuned the high-powered stereo system as Wilson and Pearson added crowning touches to the cocktail table. Their handiwork finally fallen into place, they stepped back to admire the dazzling spectacle. The paintings basked in soft radiance. Huge urns of freshly-picked, wild flowers underscored their earthiness. Every window, vase, glass and plant leaf sparkled as if someone waving a magic wand had sprinkled it all with gold dust.

There was barely time to rush home, change clothes, gulp down a light meal and get back to the gallery to open the show.

When they returned, a small crowd milled about the door. Skip Wilson, arriving first, greeted them briskly, stepping aside to let them in. They stampeded like a herd of trapped cattle, scattering fanlike straight to the bar. It was a miracle no one was crushed in the onslaught. Rex, silently surveying the proceedings, went completely undetected. Sipping his drink, he watched the formation disperse, having consumed their first transfusions and begun the next. One by one they drifted into the lofty front salon to scan the paintings. Soon the crowd stood two deep in front of each piece. Their backs often to the work, they immersed themselves as deeply into conversation as they could in the midst of bedlam.

Burt Pearson had a habit of bringing "select" personalities over to meet the artist. Rex groaned inwardly as he approached with a tall, flamboyant matron hanging on his arm. Wearing a billowy black and white print dress and wide-brimmed floppy black hat, she emerged as the colorful, outspoken art critic, Fedora Gardner. Professing devoted admiration for the "Dravus style", she harbored secret reservations. The quality of his work was evident to her "impeccable eye". But his color and imagery were a shade too realistic and finely detailed to suit her more ambiguous tastes. She greeted him effusively as if he were her closest intimate. He stoically suffered through her stream of arm waving rapture over his new show. Embarrassed for her, he steeled himself to her harangue on the previous day's preview. As he watched two fleshy protuberances move up and down, in and out, he had a curdling premonition that if he looked down her lily-white gooseneck into her putrid core he would find the soul of a shark. She fidgeted restlessly under his cold, blank stare and slunk away undaunted, spreading the latest rave tidings in her trail.

He relaxed as Dexter Crane edged his way out of a cluster of friends and headed in his direction. Having carefully cultivated a discerning reputation, the collector had two Dravus paintings as the cornerstone of his collection. In the process of acquisition, he and Rex had discovered a mutual admiration and formed a bond. Flawless in his tweed and oxford cloth, Crane strode confidently over to the aloof young giant who was like an adopted son, a kind of protégé among his artful prizes. Rex's benefactor stood before him, the patron saint who'd appeared at a time of desperate need. Freshness, a steel-trap mind and ingenuousness all registered concurrently on his solid features like images-in-triplicate on a slot machine. An oasis in the desert, Rex mused to himself, scanning the babbling horde. A passionate connoisseur of good art, he intimated to Rex his intent to add another Dravus painting to his growing concern.

Rex recognized a spotty number of serious collectors interspersed among the browsers. But the majority came to exploit an evening of free entertainment.

And then he saw her . . .

You glided regally into the room with a tall, sandy-haired woman. You were stunning, truly the most beautiful woman I'd ever seen. An eddy of enigma enveloped you as you floated through the foliage of spectators. You wore emerald green velvet, your coltish legs sheathed in deep green suede, both shades echoed in your tapestry bag. Your long hair gleamed chestnut-colored traced with copper. Your sculpted features emerged like bas-relief on a Grecian coin.

Your soul-searching eyes smoldered with unfathomable mysteries. They glanced in my direction briefly but seemed to see through and beyond me. When they alighted on mine, your stare, so intense, so piercing, bristled the hair on the back of my neck and made my shoulders shudder uncomfortably. Our eyes locked in silent communion until you lowered yours and moved on and the magic spell was broken . . .

He'd continued following her through the gallery with his eyes. Once, she turned to look at him as if she could feel the heat of their blazing intensity through her dress.

He watched as she stood for a long time before each painting, drinking in its essence, oblivious to the mayhem around her. Trancelike she drifted from painting to painting, inspecting details, scrutinizing the web of intricacies employed in their making.

They didn't speak but her eyes somehow spoke more eloquently than many voices.

After she'd hungrily devoured his oeuvre, she glanced in Rex's direction one last time, finding to her dismay that he was still studying her intently with a curious expression which she couldn't decipher completely. He wanted to know her yet, at the same time, drew a protective shield down over his features to hide behind. She left the gallery as suddenly as she'd come. Rex had never seen anything he wanted to possess more, but instinctively knew she wouldn't be easy prey using even the most exquisite lure. In a flash of perspicacity, he saw, understood, knew her, the wildest, freest spirit he'd ever encountered. She was thoroughly untamable.

After that Rex lost interest in the entire proceedings. A handful of other collectors came, were introduced, professed interest in buying and, in some cases, even backed their promises with deposits. Before long many of the title cards hanging beside the canvases sported large red dots distinguishing the sold from the unsold. The triumph did little to lift Rex's mood. He'd just fallen in love with a mysterious woman he was certain he would never see again. He wanted nothing more than to escape from the dwindling crowd and slip back into the anonymity he enjoyed in the peace and privacy of his van and Casey Banyan's studio. And he did, almost immediately after conjuring the idea. He fled with only a brief explanation to Skip Wilson and then headed straight for the Casablanca, familiar post-show watering hole. Casey, dropping by his show earlier, had such strong crowd phobia that he'd left soon after seeing the show and was already well on his way to oblivion when Rex arrived. They sat in solitary confinement most of the evening, neither wanting to be distracted from his fantasies. Rex, no matter how hard he tried, couldn't erase the image of the mysterious woman in green. Her face rose up so strikingly outlined that for one breathtaking moment he was convinced she was actually sitting in front of him.

And then she was. Standing there in her velvet finery she was even more enigmatic than his vision of her. Ethereal with the glory of copper hair, sharp features and sly glint in yellow cat-eyes, she reminded him of a cunning green fox.

By some crafty maneuvering, she managed to stay near him all evening. Never taking her eyes from his, she watched his every move, drank in his essence like a magic potion. In the stolen glances she felt purified, more strongly connected to him. They didn't need to speak. They told him everything he desired to know, held him spellbound. When her bewitching hour arrived signaling time to go, she left as unceremoniously as she'd come. And his hopes were dashed of ever seeing her again. Yet his sixth sense assured him he would, that she was not an apparition. On the contrary, she was very real, warm and alive, the enchantress he'd despaired of finding in a lifetime of pursuit, if only in his dreams. He would struggle to hold her until completely his and she chose of her own free will to come stay with him. She would, one day, he was certain...

The Dravus exhibit was proving an unqualified success. The handful of collectors on opening night had proved a very shrewd lot, quickly snapping up the most striking large canvases, realizing as crafty investors, that the prices reflected an unestablished, rising young, artistic star. And others, equally prescient, were calling, making appointments, inquiries and viewing the paintings every day. Some returned two and three times until making a final selection from the dwindling supply left unsold.

A few days before the show was to be dismantled, Rex, still camped out at Casey's studio, received the ecstatic call from Skip Wilson that would be the turning point of his career. Everything in the show had sold, the three charcoal drawings, everything. They were the sweetest words he'd ever heard or ever hoped to hear. The show was sold out. He was on his way, never to look back nor have to worry again except about maintaining the quality of the work. He and a Cheshire-grinning Casey, himself aspiring toward the Wilson/Pearson menagerie, decided the event called for another celebration. They immediately set out for the Fu Manchu Gardens, a favorite haunt of both of theirs on special occasions, that night particularly.

Entering the Fu Manchu Gardens was to be suddenly submerged into the mysteries of the deep. A surrealistic fantasy, it was strangely luminous with sea-green aquariums. The exotic interior spiraled into secret cells cubicled like a chambered nautilus's shell. Tropical trees, plants and flowers enlivened the tangled subterranean world, aglow below a serpentine string of hanging Chinese lanterns.

The two men headed for their usual back booth where Rex faced the largest tank, becoming engrossed in the aquatic antics inside. Casey, an early arrival at Rex's show, having already seen it in his studio, skirted it quickly and escaped. As they repeatedly toasted its success, he prodded Rex to reenact it from the hanging onward. Rex filled him in on the inside machinations including the tug-of-war between Wilson and Pearson over the slightest details. Surprisingly, he admitted, they usually agreed on the weightier issues. The only questions he stubbornly ignored concerned the mystery woman wrapped in emerald-green velvet.

Luckily for Rex conversing was difficult with the waiter constantly delivering steaming heaps of Chinese delicacies. Their favorite arrived, interrupting Casey's subtle probing, silencing him as his attention riveted on the quail eggs nestled in a noodle bed. Plunked down in front of him, their aroma rose to tickle his nostrils, ravishing him.

Great gobs of fried crab came smothered in black bean sauce, barbecued fish lips, ducks' feet, all crowned by the grand finale—Fu Manchu-style pork.

All the while they swigged down a steady stream of exotic drinks, potent as the dishes they accompanied. As usual, Casey was two or three glasses ahead of Rex and well on his way to Nirvana.

Hours later, stuffed and semi-conscious, the two staggered toward Casey's studio, to their surprise only a few blocks away where, once inside, they passed out on their beds.

Rex heard the phone first the next morning, almost noon, and stumbled toward it to squelch the terrible noise. It was the gallery. A reporter from the Washingtonian, the most widely circulated local newspaper, was there requesting an interview with Rex for its weekend arts column. They wanted his picture and photograph of one of his paintings from the show. And that wasn't all. The art critic, Fedora Gardner, having met him and reviewed his work, had called professing undying loyalty in her drive to spread the gospel of St. Rex. First on her agenda was convincing her contact in New York at Art/World to publish her column and accompanying picture of Rex. And, she tantalized on just before hanging up, there were her acquaintances-soon-to-be-friends at several of the major museums . . .

That was all the time he had, Skip said, to tell him any more for the moment. And there was more, he assured him. But if he was to make the interview he should come to the gallery right away. The reporter was waiting for him there.

Rex, abhorring publicity in general and reporters in particular, decided to go, for his work's sake. But it didn't turn out much better than he expected. The Washingtonian's rookie arts reviewer looked and listened half-heartedly, as if being kept from a more pressing assignation. His obtuse remarks left Rex wondering whether he'd ever seen a painting before. Only Rex's adroit fielding of the questions focused attention on more valid concerns rather than mere superficialities. But despite his vaulted efforts, he was still misquoted. He'd learned his lesson. He would never interview again. Things he'd said, almost as asides to himself, turned up in print. Any sensitive journalist listening carefully would treat them for what they were, pure hypothetical ponderings. Consequently, his descriptive analysis of the work came out sounding flatly conventional, as one-dimensional as the reporter's viewpoint. To aggravate matters, the reprint accompanying the article was the least compelling painting in the show. The rock-bottom bonus of the entire fiasco was greater exposure, if shoddy, for his art.

After that Rex refused interviews, avoiding anything to do with promotion. Critics would continue to thrust him into the spotlight, retaining a slight reserve, but he refused to be bothered, saving his energy for work.

Soon after the opening he returned to Indio Valley and his studio. But with the exhibit and attendant publicity, he was never quite as private. Calls from aficionados and admirers came often. Colleagues called with congratulations and comments. Several curators even contacted him. He referred a good deal of the callers to the gallery. His one hope was that the fuss would end with the exhibit. It did, to some extent, but not altogether.

Paint. Paint. Paint. The words thudded in his brain like a mantra chant. They pounded through him, drove him on, and delved him into the depths.

He painted maniacally. Oblivious to the furor raised by the Sealth show, he strictly disciplined himself to work long, uninterrupted stretches. Not even Rebecca's nagging demands deterred him from his quest.

The harder he worked, the more hostile and passive she grew. A wall of silence held them at bay in a hellish limbo. She'd wrapped around his persona so tightly that, in disengaging, she shriveled back into the mass of inertia she'd been, while, freed from her stranglehold, he thrived.

In the ensuing months the two, immersed in their separate ways, rarely met. Rebecca, commuting to Shetland County's Historical Museum, spent hours cataloguing significant data of local interest. Acquiring early-photographs and papers documenting the evolution of artifacts attributed to the Northwest Mukitoo tribe, the Shetland staff was in a flush of activity. Rebecca among them, classified, verified, filed the valuable cache. She arrived early and closed after everyone had gone, getting to the tiny farm long after dark, Rex worked late in the studio, stopping for a brief snack, usually after Rebecca had eaten, and disappeared again, working steadily into the night. They inhabited the same space, spasmodically, but existed in totally different realms.

Rex grew increasingly restless. Longing gnawed his insides, leaving him spent and irritable. He recognized the signs, knew them well. He knew from past experience that he was unable to harness them, unwittingly giving them free rein, aware that they were irrepressible.

He kept working but with a newly-charged energy, unchecked passion, secretly harboring deep inside the seed of discontent and the hope of eventual escape . . . .

In the long, soul-wrenching revelation to Hattie, riveting her spellbound for several hours, Rex spoke of his spirit's slow suffocation, his rebellious final hiatus with Rebecca, ultimately deserting to Gray Bar and the old beach place he now rented indefinitely.

Rex and Hattie luxuriously sighed, stretching, unraveling limbs from around each other. Basking contentedly in the crackling fire's hot glow, each mused inwardly on the mysterious string of happenstances that had brought them together, to that time and place. Given the choice, neither would wish to be anywhere, with anyone, else. It was as if destiny, like some crafty, lovelorn matchmaker, had conspired to unite them.

Exhausted, having weathered the stormy journey through Rex's past travails, they lay slumped together in a slag-heap. Limp from the mental and emotional drain, they drifted into the deepest sleep either had ever known.

After a seeming eternity they woke, feeling strangely purged of a staggering weight by their intimate night's cathartic conversation.

As their eyes retraced each other, two purified hearts, freshly impassioned, blazed out, one toward the other.

Entranced, as if suspended in time and space by the magnetic force vibrating between them, Rex slowly succumbed to the silent, unwitting summons of the yellow-green cat-eyes.

Going to her he pulled her gently up, then led her through the back door to the studio.

Inside, a riotous panoply radiated through the mullioned skylight, dappling the dirt floor with luminosity. Its powdered expanse floated up to greet them like a shimmering iridescent sea. Stillness lingered as palpable as another presence.

Rex had fashioned a straw bed in the former stall corner niche to use after late-night painting sessions.

Still holding Hattie's hand, he slowly steered her to the makeshift berth, then, releasing his clasp, turned her to him. He'd felt her stiffen, sensed her hesitancy and, as they stood face to face, saw her apprehension.

Hattie's mind and heart raced wildly.

I've listened fascinated, to your life story, stayed with you, shared your fire. I've watched every expression, every movement as you slept. I've seen your eyes sparkling with life, dance with delight, cloud over with despair. I've felt power and gentleness in your hands, sensed purpose in your stride, heard brilliance in your thoughts. I've even desired the strength and comfort of your touch, the depth and force of your passion. But still we're virtual strangers. The dark, mysterious part of you grips me with some nameless fear. Some unknown element in you keeps me from you, overwhelms, fills me with awe.

Staring intently into her curious cat-eyes, he intercepted her thoughts. His eyes answered hers with calm reassurance, belying his own confusion.

He both desired and doubted her as he could not help doubting every woman since Rebecca. His psychic wounds were just beginning to heal, his emotional armor still tender and susceptible. So soon after his resolve to lead a more temperate existence, the woman-stranger stalking his domain single-handedly stripped it away. She completely obliterated his set routine, upending his carefully ordered work pattern until all his energy and thoughts were obsessed with possessing her.

That single notion seized control, propelling him to reach out and pull her against his heaving chest. With a startled murmur, she arched back from the impact of his mouth clamping down over hers. Crushing, insistent, it lingered until her arms flew around his neck, pressing his probing lips and tongue still closer, drawing them further within hers.

Amalgamated and swaying, they clung to each other covetously.

Her shoulders tightly ensconced within his firm, leaden grip, he guided her, as she fell against him, down to the sandy floor.

His rapacious fingers roamed over her, tracing, kneading her sumptuous, velvety flesh, consumed by the possessive fury of a sculptor molding clay.

Impatient to see, feel, savor her womanly secrets, he grabbed the collar at her throat and in one deft yank, ripped off the thin sheath.

Stunned, he surveyed the rich, amber skin, incandescent beneath a filmy veil of dampness.

He was beyond the turning point even though her eyes begged him not to. His legs straddled her, pinioning her under him. He worked swiftly, unbuttoning, unzipping, to shed the disruptive barrier of his own clothing. Finally, free, he stretched full length over her, clasped her hands up over head. Seeking her mouth again he pushed it open and resumed his probing search.

Suddenly he imagined himself a deep-sea diver plummeting through the intricate mysteries of the deep—profoundly silent, splendidly arrayed. Driven to discover and conquer, he plunged with abandon ever more deeply, slowly swallowed up into the fathomless depths.

He began to sense her subtle movements beneath him. Rigid at first, her body was initiating its own response to the rhythmic fluctuations of his. Lifting and falling over her, trepidatious at first, his pace was gaining momentum, matching his buoyed spirits. Like a rising phoenix, his confidence mounted as Hattie strained to meet his steady barrage. Rocking unison, their feverish stride merged, hitting a thunderous crescendo. Finally the frenzy tapered off to a slower gait and gradually halted.

Separating at last, they embraced for a long time, not wanting or needing to speak, simply staring into one another's eyes. Intense, timorously awkward, their eyes openly mirrored wide-eyed wonderment. A shock of clairvoyance struck them as each struggled to comprehend magic.

Caught in the faceted mystique of his eyes and craving more of his protective warmth, Hattie inched over to snuggle against him.

Her heat as she pressed up against him, rubbing gently in rhythmic circles, stirred Rex's need.

She didn't purposely plan to rouse him, but only wanted to feel his nearness, reaffirm his reality. The immediacy and intensity of his rekindled desire amazed her, re-enflaming her own.

Armed with the power to incite passion and intimacy, they garnered new confidence.

Rex was intrigued and emboldened by her overtures, tentative though they were. He quickly caught up the reins, commandeering her initial cue. He needed little prodding. His body was delirious with the electricity of hers. Swaddling her within his arms' sheltering nest, he lulled her rippling body still. With lithe grace he mounted her, lunging into her swollen vessel, elusive source of her mysterious allure.

They glided lyrically as if in some ethereally draped chamber, their movements synchronized with muted, haunting strains.

Blocking out all else, they swirled, leapt and soared. In bonding they were immortal as they scaled the heights to sublimity.

Descending from such rapture, they felt a sense of irretrievable loss as they parted.

A dread of diminishing the sparks ricocheting between them held their bodies at bay, still attached midway like Siamese twins.

Reluctantly, Rex withdrew from the woman lying dreamlike beside him, careful to avoid disturbing her. Silently, in slow motion, they separated.

Quiet, touching lightly, neither ventured from that secret, beatific realm for fear of breaking the spell.

Finally Hattie stirred, threw on a tattered, plaid robe of Rex's heaped on top of work clothes laying in the corner and padded barefoot around the room. She hadn't been in the studio since first meeting Rex and was curious about the paintings making such a forceful impact.

Rex, propped against one of the ruggedly-hewn supports, studied her bemusedly as she, childlike, conducted her investigation.

Snoopy, he smiled to himself, more than a little flattered by her keen interest.

Most paintings faced the wall but that didn't deter Hattie, methodically turning them, one by one, to her lengthy scrutiny.

They're even better than I thought. There's genius in these paintings. He is great, not just good or very good, but a great artist, a brilliant, creative genius.

She responded to some more strongly than others, but overall they were of consistently high quality with a great degree of mastery. To her mind, heart, eyes and ears they flowed, sparkled, sang.

And when she looked at Rex again he saw not only love and admiration but a kind of reverent homage.

Unable to repress her emotional flood-tide, she raced to him. He caught her up just as she hurled her body into his outstretched arms.

Helpless to resist the torrent of ardor threatening to consume them, they recklessly let it run rampant.

The following days and nights, sleeping and eating scantily, they drew sustenance from the wellspring of their sated desires.

They made no promises, didn't rush to map out any future blueprint. They were both too newly liberated from former misalliances. The headiness of their hard-won emancipation rendered them as giddy as newborn foals. They felt no urgent need, as they once had with others, to hurry into another bondage that might prove difficult to reverse.

Both harbored secret doubts about indulging in the luxury of caring with abandon. Neither felt ready for anything more for the moment.

For as long as either could remember, taking pride in the achievement, unfettered independence was top priority. Trespassing or disruption of those hallowed grounds posed a dangerous threat. Inviolability was assured by sidestepping anything upsetting that equilibrium. Like the law of the wilderness, it was the battle for survival of every living, wild creature to insure its liberty and continuity. The crucial difference between the artist's untameability and an animal's centered on the first's right of free artistic expression. Any constriction of emotional or intellectual faculties might hamper the scope and acuity of vision. Any interruption or mitigation of the imagination's flow fostered concern. Hattie and Rex, two veterans of adversity, had long been seasoned in the art of survival. Deftly they sniffed out and dodged anything or anyone bent on obstructing their progress, or impinging their exploration of the utmost reaches of experience. Each had hardened to the difficult sacrifices made for the sake of art. More than once that surrender had been, for both, in the form of a person. Rebecca's paranoia had erected a hefty barrier between Rex and his destiny. Just as ruthlessly, he'd cast her from his life and thoughts like an old pair of shoes. Hattie had discarded Murdoch, ridding herself of his manipulation until she breathed fresh air again. She'd never felt so deliciously clean and free as the day she'd left him and driven to the ocean.

Since her childhood in Odessa, she'd cultivated a rugged individualism nourished by her secret life in the wilds, utterly separate from the one she lived with her family. They knew little, if anything, about her love affair with the woods, with every river, stream, wildflower, insect, plant and animal in her path. At home she blended into the background as benignly as a piece of furniture. She was mild, quiet, didn't upset the monotonous rhythm or cause the slightest wave. Instead she cloaked her restlessness in a mantle of feigned docility. Burying her famished curiosity in books, she spent hours rifling through the library's shelves. She read, listened to mystery programs on the radio, watched movies, sketched horses, colored pictures, drew. But her heart was never in them. Instead her imaginings floated out to the haunting wilderness, its mysteries, its exquisite surprises beckoning her. It was as if she were some hunted beast whose first mating call came, not from a male member of her species, but, from the forest itself. And she gravitated to it as to a rendezvous with a forbidden lover whenever possible.

As she matured, Hattie nurtured her spirit as she would fertilize a secret garden. She protected and defended her freedom as fiercely as she would her own offspring. Her conviction about the inalienability of independence only grew stronger with time. She learned that wild things attract other wild things, are drawn to them in return and that a spark of recognition ignited between them.

That dynamic had exerted its will over her and Rex. Affinity, mirrored in the eyes of their twin spirits, registered instantly with the shock and drama of spontaneous combustion.

The rare chance of meeting a kindred nature escaped neither of them. It only heightened the experience, enhanced its essence. They savored the moment of mutual discovery, relishing it like a succulent meal. Their greatest concern was to preserve it somehow, prolong the magic.

And they had. Coming together completely for the first time in the studio, there had been magic between them. Rex mused to himself:

More magical than first seeing her in the gallery. Even more magical than meeting her again at the beach when she stopped to look at my painting.

He never wanted the magic between them to end. But he feared it would as it had so abruptly vanished between him and Rebecca. That perplexing element, when gone, was gone forever, never to be revived, leaving only bitterness and despair in its wake. Its nature was so fragile that it disappeared completely when he was with Rebecca and he despaired of ever knowing it again.

Since Hattie, not only his spirits, but also his hope of its reincarnation were reborn. The headlines flashed across the front page of his mind:

THE MIRACULOUS RENAISSANCE OF MAGIC. MAGIC MAKES A REMARKABLE COMBACK.

Possessed of uncanny magnetic force, her essence was slowly mingling with his own, burrowing under his skin until it felt as if its current had set his blood on fire. Unwittingly the copper-tressed stranger had ingratiated her way so fully into his mind that every conjured fantasy bore her stamp.

His traitorous thoughts dwelt solely on the yellow-eyed vixen even while working, especially while working. Those once malleable thoughts, royally besotted, preferred wallowing in murky images of the she-devil.

Each time her visage cropped up it was as if his mental wires had been short-circuited into focusing on her. Fighting desperately to shrug it off, his sudden desire for her consumed him so strongly that he would have to stop working and find her.

He left the studio and walked over to the house. He found Hattie in the master bedroom they shared since first making love in the studio.

She was curled up in the window-seat she'd fashioned out of pillows and an old quilt and which looked out to the sea. She was intently absorbed in a book nestled in her lap. When Rex came in her head reared up as she eyed him suspiciously. She never expected to see him during his working hours. But there he was with set jaw and passionate fierceness in his eyes.

She'd never looked so beautiful. Her copper hair fell loosely about her swanlike neck, stopping just before her shoulders. She was wrapped in a velvet lounging gown of pale violet.

Pulling her from her perch, he loosed the tie. Her unleashed contours sprang toward him in naked profusion as if to orchestrate the strong, firm strokes of his impresario's touch.

With skilled mastery of his subject, his hands glided over each silken curve, well enough versed on her body's instrument to elicit the desired responses. The swiftness of its reaction to his sensitive, probing fingers momentarily stunned her. She pressed her body forcefully against his, causing them to swagger back until he had a chance to steady himself and his hold on her. Once righted he continued to explore the lush terrain that never ceased to fascinate him. Fueling his imagination to a raging pitch, her fragrance ignited his desire every time they touched. But it was her haunting mystique, shrouded in intrigue, that utterly bewitched him.

Gripping her to him, he inched back to the high four-poster and lay her across it. Stripping off her tangled robe, he gathered her to him, reeling above her arching frame. Her hunger for him was as urgent as his for her. Fused together, one form seared into the other's flesh like a hot iron branding its quarry.

Never before Hattie, had Rex felt such a fierce intangible craving, a deep surge within to be matched in intensity and quelled.

The force's gathering momentum frightened him. But even more dismaying was knowing its catalyst was his mounting obsession with the woman before him. Wary of anyone possessing that much power over him, he secretly warned himself to beware. He would not be controlled, trapped into submission or surrender, especially not by the woman for whom he'd begun to care so deeply. He would disguise the full extent of his devotion to protect his own interests.

Hattie's antennae picked up a subtle shift in his mood, the psychological warfare plaguing him with which he was desperately trying to grapple. But unaware she might be the cause, that her body's ambrosia acted like an aphrodisiac on his, she was more than a little puzzled. She knew only the brilliance, magnetism, potency embedded in his every fiber, and, being the product of such munificence, he symbolized the quintessential male.

She could not encompass him fully enough. His elusive nature seemed to forever hover just beyond her reach. Yet his body valiantly tried to resist the soothing oasis of hers. He wouldn't let himself be ambushed without a fight.

His retreat confused her. Only moments before he'd been the epitome of unrestrained passion. But then he withdrew, seeking shelter beneath some kind of impenetrable shell as if to hibernate.

His strange behavior completely mystified her. He seemed to be toying with her. His little game of hide and seek was beginning to pall and she was growing exasperated. At times it seemed his single objective was railroading her to take the initiative. It occurred to her that his odd ways could be subconscious, his motives innocent. Still, she didn't understand his need to bend her will to him.

The only reason she deduced was that his pride kept him from appearing to grovel before a woman. A proud, stubborn man, he was deeply rooted in some prehistoric code that forbade him any emotional displays. Evidently the code's first rule was never acquiesce to the woman. It seemed by the mandates of that illusory creed, that the woman's place was at his feet, waiting to be tapped on the shoulder to rise and worship him.

Rex, to Hattie one of the code's greatest adherents, intimated he would stand his ground, that she must come to him.

His stoicism was corroding the magic they had first shared. It was capable of mutilating the noble, honest foundation upon which their first union had been based.

Her own stubborn pride further threatened their lofty ideal. But she couldn't help it. It just wasn't in her nature to succumb to tyranny, no matter what form, even the subtlest coercion.

Their love's new bud was already tainted, being silently invaded by foreign elements, its potential flowering jeopardized.

The great expectancy both lovers harbored to finally embrace the grand passion of a lifetime, was waning rapidly.

Their initial delirium, once moving full steam, had reached an impasse.

But despite the mercurial undercurrent treading between them, the inert corpus of animal magnetism resurged. They came together devoid of ulterior motive or nagging doubt, not because they wanted to but because they needed to. Their natural course, predetermined at the outset, was destined to converge at the present crossroads. The dilemma of which way to take didn't deter them. Blindly led by their hearts' upheaval, they bushwhacked a path out of primal instincts, leaving the road of reason far in the dust.

Their self-imposed barriers were swiftly dismantled, the weighty issue of liberty temporarily skirted. Rex, his body poised to thrust, lunged and plunged, ravishing Hattie over and over. He seemed unable to get enough of her and she couldn't seem to get her fill of him. His ravaged face hovering over, she reached up to trace its crevices, carving a vision of it in her mind. Her fingers brushed over the windswept tuft above his mouth, played across his lips, moving down to stroke the soft bramble bush of beard. Their glazed eyes echoed their bodies' need. Unflinching, he detected a tinge of awe, while she saw his searching question.

Later, as they lay entangled, a hoard of brooding thoughts flooded their brains:

Where are we headed? Where will it end? What does everything between us mean? Is it genuine? Will it last? Is the feeling between us real or merely fleeting, an empty infatuation? Now we're rootless, two vagabonds, wild things, free to roam randomly. Do we belong together, can we preserve our spirits' freedom, keep our souls untamed, in tact, or must we part? Are intimacy and independence compatible or are they mutually exclusive, canceling each other out? Should we go separate ways? Are we better off alone? Or is this magic too exquisite to know again? And if we chose to abandon it, have we already gone too far to let go?

They clutched each other closely, gripped more tightly; afraid the doubts scuttling through their minds might be detected.

The only recourse was to give their hearts free rein, let them lead the way, flow along in a natural rhythm. They were together, superbly situated, deliciously suited. Time would decide. If they were patient, the box full of mysteries threatening to usurp their bond might be unlocked, the truth unmasked.

Their minds were so in sync that they reached the same conclusion in silent accord. Weightless, they stretched, unflexed their bodies with sheer relief. They could proceed unhampered by any misgivings. Nature could continue her course uninterrupted by them. They would patiently persist. They would watch and wait.

Their days were filled with endless walks along the beach, horseback riding, fireside readings, painting. Putting up an easel at one end of the studio, Hattie set to work. Her newfound contentment was reflected in her paintings. She began slowly, keeping small-scale at first, since she hadn't worked regularly for so long. Gradually a new confidence and maturity began to seep in, reflected in the strong, authoritative style. She started with a suite of mid-size canvases. Anything less caused claustrophobia, constricting her vision. The longer she worked the more she realized how much she'd missed painting, the void it had caused in her life, how great a part of her it was.

Her pace increased, the current favorable conditions spurring her surge of creativity. The beach's wild beauty inspired many of the paintings, its power and abundance willing her imagination to transcend mundanity.

Even its sounds were more profound, unlike other places-seagull cries, incoming tide, whirring wind through wild sea grass-unique, familiar, comforting, elevating and expanding her thoughts to embrace eternity. A smattering of skeletons, bones, shells, petrified wood, marked rocks served as symbols of primeval mysteries.

Painting stirred a fever again, pouring forth laden with the elemental force of surf crashing against the cliffs. Urged on by the surrounding magic, brush in hand, she quickened the rhythm from palette to canvas, rapidly daubing on the pigment. Her fingers flew to encapsulate a single moment of the ephemeral scene before her. Soon the paintings sparkled ebulliently with a lyricism most of her previous work, lackluster from missing ingredients, had only hinted.

Life resurged dramatically, flooding each new work. She felt the difference as she went, saw some beauteous metamorphosis on the canvas, as rising juices rejuvenated her spirit. The sudden breakthrough overwhelmed her as if she were in the throes of some mystic revelation. Yet she interpreted it not in the religious sense but rather as the renaissance of her artistic powers.

Undetected, Rex watched the drama unfold in Hattie and her work. It was a facet of her he hadn't witnessed before. The sphinxlike creature he beheld looked as if she'd suddenly turned to stone, intensely concentrated, completely unaware of his existence. Inner strength and confidence governed each sure, deliberate mark. Every touch of the brush glided as if possessed of unwavering purpose. Never faltering nor slackening, she moved to the beat of her inner rhythm, fully charged, driven, obsessed.

At first, as he observed Hattie's conversion from wobbly, spindle-legged neophyte into sure-footed dynamo, Rex was more than a trifle piqued. A good portion of the passionate energy once showered upon him she channeled into the radiant offspring emerging, one by one, in a steady stream. But his heart was soon captivated, his soul conquered. Together in concert, triumphant, they irrefutably won him over, their reverent servant, obediently transfixed in mind and spirit.

He silently pledged to reactivate his voluminous store of patience. It was her time for untrammeled solitude to hone her visual voice. Staving off any selfish interests, he vowed to stay on the sidelines until the moment was ripe for her to rediscover him.

He didn't begrudge the wait. Intrigued, he fascinatedly observed the restless virago scale the heights of her powers.

She'd never felt so free, charged or more fully tried than while pursuing the new paintings. They were the sum, the fruit of her essence. They were the totems of her nomadic sojourns, the harvest of her relentless sowing. Entombed within them lay the markings, signs and symbols of all the mysteries that had stirred her. And still they were only one branch of her trek through the forest of unfathomable secrets toward the source of enlightenment.

The more they were together, the better Hattie and Rex understood the complex nature of freedom.

Above all, each craved a strong passionate love, shared intimacy, yet at the same time held ferociously onto the sanctity of a rugged individualism not to be sacrificed for anything or anyone. All invaders of that domain or challenging its preeminence would be ostracized. Rex and Hattie, following their maxim, were survivors, two freedom fighters emerging from the mercenary jungle around them. Soon each had recognized a kindred spirit in the other, knew dangerous infractions like boundaries overstepped would not be committed.

They went into the studio every morning and set up their easels. Hattie purposely chose the side closest to the sea as her designated post. For as long as she could remember, something deep inside her started to wither and die whenever she ventured too far from the water. So in Rex's studio where she'd begun to feel so secure, she instinctively gravitated to the western wall to work. Hearing the surf swish onto the beach, she was both transported and becalmed. She was gentled, almost tamed, by its might.

Through the weathered walls the song of the waves racing and breaking played on, mesmerizing her so that her rhythm fell in step with its windblown beat, lapsing into a steady, easy gait. Something of its wild, beckoning melody ingrained itself into her spirit's inner chambers. She was inwardly regaining her natural stride, knew that somehow she had chanced upon her rightful place in the scheme of things. But for how long? And what then or where? And with whom? Would it still be Rex? If she left would he be willing to leave what he too might regard as his natural place? For the present they were content in their secluded niche and more productive than either had been in recent times.

Then why would either of us abandon so potent a setting where our work is flourishing; a place where we feel comfortable, productive, a huge expansive place, nurturing, conducive to both art and passion? Could anyplace we go from here match its magic, its memories, poetic beauty or drama? Does its equal exist and, if so, where?

But, her sixth sense already detected signs of unrest in Rex's manner, mood, conversation and, most noticeably, his work. He acted like a man on the warpath.

Something was slowly eroding his equilibrium. He didn't say anything or reveal much, but her sensory antennae registered his growing malaise. Stymied by his sudden, mysterious brooding, she resolved to decipher his discontent or at least try. His remoteness mystified and alienated her but she would not be excluded without more than a little resistance. His passion for her was just as fervent but she felt the change when only his body responded. His mind, his spirit eluded her, thwarted her efforts to conquer him.

Keeping their distance while working wasn't new but gradually the breach grew beyond the studio, spilling over into their private realm. Rex withdrew even further into his fantasy-world and quietly shut the door. Hattie suffered the impact of his retreat just as acutely as if it had been more overt. Again he became the silent, puzzling creature he was when they first met. Again she found herself with a stranger in a strange land. He did nothing to narrow the widening schism between them, seemingly unaware of her mounting despair or that anything might be amiss.

Rex's apparent oblivion was deftly orchestrated. His feigned indifference, artfully honed over time as protection from enemies, made skillful use of the same subtle mechanism a chameleon employs to confound a predator.

But his complex maneuvers weren't well enough disguised to keep Hattie from feeling the sharp sting of rejection. To her, his message, however convoluted, was clear. Keenly she felt like an interloper just when their intimacy seemed headed toward sublimity. But Rex was already retreating, leaving her stranded in the wilderness to fend for herself and she felt powerless to keep him. Inwardly she called to him, reached out to him but he was beyond hearing or caring.

He sensed her distress, her aching need, felt her yearning but some greater force gripped him, drove him on, controlled his movements. His renegade thoughts were on the rampage as well. Unable to rein them in, he had no recourse but to let them run free. They kept straying back to the Indio Valley, the farm, the studio, and the land, retracing magical adventures but were forbidden to dwell on Rebecca.

Working together as usual in the studio, he and Hattie drifted further apart. Sometimes, feeling suddenly strange, she would look up to find Rex standing stock-still intently surveying her. Embarrassed at being apprehended he turned back to his work, leaving her more bewildered than before. She dared not believe what her eyes glimpsed.

That faraway fleeting look filled with exquisite tenderness—haunting ruefulness or purely imagined? Momentarily it seems he might step across his precious barrier and call a truce. Could it be or is it only another daydream? Merely a mirage? Probably. Possibly . . . .

Every subsequent day followed a pattern set during the recent past—a withering erosion spoiling the magic they'd just begun to know.

Little by little, they witnessed the ebbing of a once frenzied ardor. It waned until the flowing current listed, drifting aimlessly almost to a standstill.

Day by day Hattie buried herself deeper in work seeking solace, licking her wounds, smoothing her ruffled pride. The fading specter of their lust reignited, pouring forth from Rex's pent-up storehouse in a frenetic outpouring of exquisite new work.

Revitalized by the nourishing sap previously saved for Hattie, his creative powers rose and fell with the same force as the incoming tide.

Suddenly, more inspired than even before Hattie, his subconscious, beyond trivial concerns, braved the intoxicating realm he'd once only skirted, where only a few intrepid souls dared venture.

Clearly his work had suffered since his break with Hattie, but it once again became the focal point of his existence. He no longer whiled away his painting time on her.

His creative drive was full steam again, nearly as strong as before his rocky private life corroded his emotional spirit. Rebecca had adversely affected his productivity, stormily snowballing her poisonous residue into his intimacy with Hattie. It festered and erupted, near disintegration until Rex began venturing beyond the sanctity of Hattie's rarefied world.

And Hattie helplessly watched him slipping away.

Since his show he'd stayed with the Wilson/Pearson Gallery. Gradually Hattie's art came to their attention. They offered her a one-woman show of recent work, the strongest to date.

Like Rex, to circumvent their collapsing romance, she poured herself full throttle into her art. Painting constantly, she issued forth more compelling work than before.

Her subdued palette suggested a somber mood, but its tone was also softer, gentler, more reflective. She'd sunk blood and sinew into their becoming. Poetry suffused the near life-size canvases. Another dimension surfaced that had only been suggested in the earlier ones. Far greater depth and mystique permeated the finely honed strata of each newborn.

Something unexpected shone through the luminous surfaces, a subtle enigma more elusive than ever.

She could only paint—more, better, longer—delving even deeper.

She wanted only to work. It reflected her intensified commitment, dedication, conviction. Everything about her latest creations was more convincing. Since the slow death of her life with Rex, her work had leapt forward with renewed vigor. It became the reliquary for all her surplus passion.

Richer, more complex, they alluded to ancient mysteries through signs and symbols carved from the sinew of her soul. Semi-recognizable forms resembled arrowheads, cuneiforms, reliefs, assorted artifacts, vessels and fossillike imprints. Something surrealistic, almost mystical, shaded the painted shapes. Each embodied a mood, feeling, vision transposed from her soul's innards into a correspondingly significant symbol.

By then Hattie had appropriated the studio exclusively for her use. Rex, pursuing a different direction in his painting, was always working out in the field. Early every morning he loaded up his van with canvas, paints, brushes, then headed down the road in search of just the right spot to set up his easel.

But instead of painting he brooded over the state of his affairs.

What was amiss? How did it go away? Where had he run amok?

He loved Hattie as he'd loved no other woman. She, to him, was woman incarnate, embodying the best of all the women he'd ever known. She was all women, she *was* woman, *the* woman of his dreams. She had come to life, wanted him above all others, to be loved by him alone. And he seemed capable only of sabotaging their love's survival. He didn't know why, nor how to halt its downstream momentum, just that he must try. Mostly he wanted to try to reverse the collision course they were on. It was more than he'd known a few hours before.

Since knowing Hattie, he'd come to learn the extent of her deep-seated attachment to the sea . . . it seemed to be an obsession. He'd reached the conclusion that his sole rival was nothing more than a body of water. And yet so much more than a *mere* anything. He realized it would be virtually impossible to pull her away from the sea's great allure. He remembered how she punctuated her conversation with allusions to its spell over her. Many times she'd referred to her life-long desire to be near it, conditioned as she was by her frequent childhood visits. She emphatically recounted endless frustrations, numerous obstacles she'd surmounted to be by it again. Always imploring eyes met his, begging him not to come between them as had, on so many occasions, so many times before. It wasn't only integral to her existence; the subliminal thread binding her limbs, tissues and organs together. But more, it had become the chief source of her anima's renewal.

The sea, her lifeblood, was his rival . . . he knew he couldn't entice her from its mystery, was no match for its eternal grandeur. She was as inevitably linked to it as the moon was to the rise and fall of the tides. Its multitudinous moods were mirrored in the quixotic fluctuations of hers. It even seemed to him as if her unpredictability were colored by the sea's current state. He began to discern a direct correlation in their rhythms. When it lay calm and serene, she was subdued. When it tossed stormily, she, too, rose up in rebellion. They lay fallow together, they raged simultaneously. And all its cyclical vacillations, cloaked, veiled and draped as they were in surreal mystery and supreme beauty, were matched measure for measure by the vicissitudes of her own restless nature.

Despairing of ever sharing the lofty place it held in her heart, Rex waged a campaign strategy of his own. He was obsessed with teaching her that he was in charge, which led to more angst in the wake of his omnipotent rival. His own tempestuous nature only exacerbated his maneuvers. In his frustration he would nearly lose control of his faculties. He thrust out a spew of vicious words in a voice foreign even to himself, lashing Hattie with them like a whip. They were foul, brutally cutting her to the quick as he'd intended:

"You bitch..."
"You whore..."
"You Indian slut..."

"I'll never marry you now. You're so confused you don't even know if you want me. Your priorities are all mixed up. You're more in love with that damned ocean than you are with me. Well you can have your fucking ocean. Why are you here? You're not in love with me. No! You're only in love with *it*. Well you can fucking well have it. Why? Why? *WHY?*

And he ranted on until he was red-faced and gasping. Then, taking the drink he was holding, with a great upward heave, he threw a blast of it in her face, and another, and another until her hair was wet and strings of it fell across her face momentarily blinding her.

Stunned by the brute force of his venomous attack she staggered backwards. She knew only that she must escape from the pain he increasingly inflicted.

The less control he felt he held over her, especially her mind, the more enraged he grew until their relationship had splintered into regular bouts of violence. He'd never hit her but each eruption came nearer the striking zone. She felt helpless against his irrational tirades and more despairing.

Every time they argued he attacked not only her but her paintings, the same paintings he supposedly held in such high esteem. When enraged he referred to them as those "lousy decorator paintings". He was sure then that he'd hurt her to the core. He was like a frenzied shark feeding on the bloodletting he'd incurred.

He was right in his assumption. She was devastated. Never fully able to hide her feelings, she felt and looked wretchedly heartsick.

It was all eroding into a rocky roller coaster ride and she could barely muster enough energy to disembark.

As self-protection, Hattie had slowly built a barrier of icy reserve. Her life's blood felt as though it had turned to salt, her body into stone. Seeing it would be futile to try penetrating it to reach her, Rex's blazing fury was reignited.

Dead were her idyllic dreams of peace, harmony, truth and beauty for their life together. The bright rays reigning down on them were long gone. If she were ever to experience them again it would have to be by taking another road. The one less traveled perhaps, but, for the solitary, it was the only one left open.

She felt the lonely waif stranded in a quagmire of muck, lost in the wilderness struggling to find the way out.

The great love of her life was shattering into a million tiny shards of nothingness, a simmering volcano suddenly fuming to life.

And where would she venture? How far and long? She'd been on the move all her life, a gypsy seeking shelter from the storm-tossed sea of her own being, craving solace but finding only more tempests along the way.

She needn't go much further. She was near the sea. It beckoned and she heard. She was there and this time she was home to stay.

THE END

www.ingramcontent.com/pod-product-compliance
Lightning Source LLC
LaVergne TN
LVHW091603060526
838200LV00036B/972